T0194069

HIS TIMELESS TOUCH

Twelve Remarkable Short Stories of
Lives Changed by the Healer.

DEBBY L. JOHNSTON

WESTBOW
PRESS®
A DIVISION OF THOMAS NELSON
& ZONDERVAN

DLJ logo by Kate Frick.

Scripture taken from the King James Version of the Bible.

This is a work of fiction. All of the characters, names, incidents,
organizations, and dialogue in this novel are either the products
of the author's imagination or are used fictitiously.

WestBow Press books may be ordered through booksellers or by contacting:

WestBow Press
A Division of Thomas Nelson & Zondervan
1663 Liberty Drive
Bloomington, IN 47403
www.westbowpress.com
1 (866) 928-1240

ISBN: 978-1-9736-4061-5 (sc)
ISBN: 978-1-9736-4062-2 (hc)
ISBN: 978-1-9736-4060-8 (e)

Library of Congress Control Number: 2018911309

Print information available on the last page.

WestBow Press rev. date: 10/23/2018

Reader Comments on Debby's Other Books:

"Debby's characters have imperfections, hopes, and dreams. Her easy style keeps you engaged and ready for more." – E. Hall

"Very inspiring!" – V. Woodrum

"Debby's books are a breath of fresh air and a delight to read!" – M. Merry

Other books by Debby:

The Cherish Novel Series:
Cherish: A Still, Small Call
Cherish: Behold, I Knock
Cherish: Create in Me a Clean Heart

CONTENTS

FOREWORD

Ask a librarian to write a foreword, and you are likely to be confronted with the jargon and peculiarities of library science. Worldcat assigns the subject "Jesus Christ—Fiction" to nearly 6,000 items in its capacious holdings; a significant but small number alongside the more than 200,000 items under the broader subject heading "Jesus Christ." Fiction on the life of Jesus is a reputable topic, and can boast both classic titles (*Ben Hur, In His Steps,* and *Pilgrim's Progress,* among many) and well-known authors (Robert Graves, Lew Wallace, Anne Rice). This book adds to that number.

If some (disciples or no) should ask as at Matthew 26:9, "To what purpose?" the verse following informs us: not only that "Jesus understood," but he also acknowledged "she hath wrought a good work upon me."

Not that you would find Debby Johnston seeking in some way the distinction of any of the Biblical women possible (Mary, Martha's sister? Mary Magdalene?) as the one long remembered for her gift of perfume; but this book, like that of the anonymous woman, is also a gift of love.

The reverence of evangelicals for Scripture is not limited to the Protestant slogan "Sola Scriptura." It is also embodied in the title of Hankey and Fischer's hymn, "I Love to Tell the Story." And it is shaped in the pastoral retelling of the Gospel. Debby's collection of short stories in this volume brings all these functions together.

Anachronism plays an important function in these tales. I recall an early brush with the technique from the pulpit; though a born critic, I found myself tickled by a pastor who described Genesis 12:5 as Abram packing up his possessions and relatives, then setting out to Canaan—in an RV. The picture came too fresh, too startling, too humorous, to offend or outrage the historical sense. Of course, there were no combustion engines in Palestine until near the turn of the last century; but far from diminishing perspective onto the ancient world, the juxtaposition of the recreational vehicle on Abram's wanderings made the call of God—on that unthinkably remote time—come into sudden focus.

Nagel and Wood's apology for anachronism as "neither an aberration nor a mere rhetorical device, but a structural condition" [Nagel, Alexander, and Christopher S. Wood. "Interventions: Toward a New Model of Renaissance Anachronism." *Art Bulletin* 87, no. 3 (September 2005): 403-415)] deserves more broad application than simply to 15-century artists. In these stories, Debby's deliberate strategy tells the "old, old story" in the 21st century; never mind that the names of principal figures most often match their authorized version context. This historical repositioning bids fair to create a vivid encounter with Scripture, and with Scripture's singular Author.

May you also find your mind's stories reinvigorated in these timeless stories, in the fresh settings Debby has wrought them in.

In Christ,

Don Day
Director of Library and Information Services
B. H. Carroll Theological Institute

Letter From The Author

Dear Friend,

Over my reading career I have been Nancy Drew, Huckleberry Finn, and Velvet Brown, among others, and I have lived in virtually every state and many countries.

In a similar way, I have been the fisherman Peter, the lad with the loaves and fishes, and the blind Bartimaeus. Sunday school teachers, preachers, and illustrated Bible storybooks stirred my spiritual imagination, early on, and shaped for me the story of Jesus.

And I'm still learning. I love hearing and reading God's Word because God is an author like no other, and no other story breathes the life everlasting.

It is out of this love for the Word that I offer my short story collection. Like twelve sermon illustrations, the goal of each juxtaposition from New Testament times to our modern day is to put us at the feet of Jesus. It is there we discover, as did the disciples, that Jesus is, indeed, the son of God.

My stories are in no way a replacement for Scripture—any more than a preacher intends for his sermon illustrations to replace your study of the Bible. It is my desire that each fictionalized account urges you to recheck the Biblical account from which it is drawn. To help you do that, I've included a *Scripture Index* and a *Bible Character Index*. Nothing would make me happier than to know I've stirred you to read the original story.

On that same note, I hurry to say I do not believe this book is appropriate for traditional Bible study. However, because it may prove valuable for reader discussion, I have provided a *Reader's Discussion Guide* with some of my thoughts in composing each retelling.

Yes, I have introduced additional characters and contemporary backgrounds, but the Scriptural Jesus I relate does not vary from the Master who walked, talked, and touched the lives of Thomas, Matthew, Peter, and John. I believe you will distinguish clearly between Biblical fact and my fiction. But if you have any question, please reference the *Scripture Index* and look up the actual Gospel accounts.

I pray the important take-away from each story is Jesus, the indisputable son of God, who came to earth with life-giving power to redeem us from sin and secure our eternity with him. That is the only message worth examining!

May the timeless Jesus touch your heart, today.

Debby

Dedicated with all praise to our risen Jesus Christ, who is the same yesterday, today, and forever.

1

PART OF HIS COMPANY

Part One

"Thomas!"

I smile. My little sister's cry of surprise greets me at the door of our dad's house and culminates in a smother of hugs.

Lisa is my favorite sibling. When the others moved out to start their families, Lisa remained. Instead of marrying, she stayed to keep house for Dad. I admire her for that. And as always, she recognizes and respects my mood. I came out of the womb moody (unlike my twin). Lisa senses I'm not ready to talk about my return home. For now, she doesn't push. It is enough I am here.

"Dad will be home, soon," she says, and as we sit, the tinkle of ice in our glasses laces our silence. Lisa's tea cools my insides, and the air-conditioner cools the rest of me.

It's hot for spring in our high-desert locale, and I'm recovering from my ride home. It wasn't a long trip, but I had somehow managed to hitch a ride in what must be the only non-air-conditioned car in the country. I had sweated and flapped in the torrid blast for untold miles with windows down and dust in my teeth. I made myself sit, now, instead of impolitely rushing upstairs for a shower.

Sitting at the kitchen table floods me with memories of dinners and lively discussions over Mom's pot roast and peach pie. From the youngest to the oldest, my siblings and I were encouraged to engage in expressing our opinions on current events, religious controversies, and the activities of our lives. Invariably, voices would be raised, Dad would shout it all down, and Mother would escape to the kitchen to wring out her sentiments on a dishcloth or unsuspecting towel.

Lisa was one of the quieter ones, but she could hold her own when it was necessary. Now, in a low voice she says, "Dad called you a fool after you left. But he grew proud of you. He would brag on you to our city cousins and say, 'My boy is part of Jesus's inner circle, you know.'"

She looks up, now, hoping for a smile. But I can't. I don't respond.

My little sister has used the word *fool*. I don't feel like a fool, but I do feel betrayed. After all that has happened, I can only imagine what she and Dad must think. But I want to save my story—the story of the last three years of my life—for when Dad arrives. I want to tell it only once.

How fast the time has flown. It seems like yesterday I was saying goodbye. When I left this house, I was young at heart, and Jesus was a virtual stranger. I had been drawn to go with him. And I marvel, now, that even though I had never been away from home, my father held his peace. Dad respected my choice. Jesus, a rising religious teacher and healer, would mentor me and eleven other students in a tour bus that would go wherever Jesus directed. And since then, the bus has introduced Jesus to thousands of people in hundreds of venues.

My favorite stop will always be the one two years ago that brought me back here. I was so excited to come home, and I remember thinking:

> *I know this road! I can't believe we've turned here. To go left at the crossroads would have taken us far away, but this road leads home. Jesus pointed right, and Peter turned the wheel.*
>
> *At the edge of town, the bus stops for gas, and while Peter pumps and Judas pays, I jump out and race ahead on foot. I can't contain my excitement. This is my town, and these are my people. I want Jesus to meet and touch them all.*

"Jesus is here!" I bellow abroad like Paul Revere, up Sycamore Street, across to Maple Avenue, and then back down Beech Street—the boundaries of my old neighborhood.

Heads pop up everywhere, and friends sprint after me. Some run to collect family members, and others flock at my back. Jesus's fame has preceded him, and no one dares miss the chance to see, hear, or touch him.

Lisa leans out from the porch and waves. I blow her a kiss before she runs inside to fetch Dad.

Old Fred Padget tosses away the morning paper and springs from his porch swing. "Where?" he cries, and I yell, "The courthouse lawn!" (It will be hard for Fred to lift Daisy with her lifeless legs, but I am sure she will soon be on her way downtown in their big yellow Chevy.)

Russ Loomis's car slows when he passes me. "Go to the courthouse, Russ," I holler. "Jesus will be there!" Russ bobs his head, wheezes his lung-cancer cough, and executes a speedy U-turn.

Katy Elm jogs on foot after snatching up her sightless baby and popping her into a stroller.

I've set a brisk pace and exult when the crowd jostling at my back gets to the Square before Jesus does. The Master's usual entourage (dozens of vehicles filled with groupies from places Jesus has already been) begins to clog the streets that lead to the town's center. If we hadn't arrived first we would have been consigned to the outer edges of the action.

While waiting on the lawn, I preen like a peacock. My dad treats me with respect; he lets me be in charge. And my friends ask things like, "What is Jesus like? Will we get to touch him? Since we're with you, will we get closer to him? Does Jesus really heal people? Will Lily Elm or Daisy or Russ get healed, today?"

My reminiscence dissolves in the bang of the kitchen door. Dad is home; somehow, I failed to hear his car pull in. I nervously stand to accept his clap on my shoulder.

"Welcome home!" Dad booms out. And I am fine until he steps back and looks me in the eye. "Are you okay, son?"

That's all it takes. I break down and sob, "No, I'm not okay."

I fight the weeping. Lisa leads me to the living room and seats me in a chair.

Between my tearful convulsions, I say, "I assume you've seen the news. Jesus has been executed. I guess it's all over. And I've come home."

I don't know what I expected, but my dad, not given to outpourings of compassion and empathy, pats my shoulder.

"I know it's hard, son," he says. "The world tends to kill prophets who say things people in power don't want to hear. I'm glad you're safe. We've spent the last two days worrying about you."

In a momentary twinge of guilt, I recognize that my decision to come home had little to do with alleviating their worry. I have come home to run away.

Lisa asks, "Are the others safe?"

Her question is a good one. I don't really know, but I say, "I think they are. When I left, they were talking about going home, too. But they planned to lie low until things settled and made it safer to travel. I took the chance and came home, now."

"I'm glad you did," Lisa says. And I sigh because I think she interprets it as bravery.

Dad now assumes his in-charge air and says, "Ever since you joined with Jesus, Lisa and I have followed the news about him. And sometimes we would catch sight of you on television. But with so many questionable reports, it was hard to decide what was true. If Jesus hadn't visited our town, and I hadn't seen with my own eyes how he healed our friends, I wouldn't have understood why you stayed with him and why the crowds followed him."

Then Dad says, "I still have trouble with reports that Jesus raised somebody from the dead."

He looks at me over his glasses as if to say, "That's an exaggeration, right?"

I manage to reply steadily, "That's true, Dad. Jesus did raise someone from the dead."

Dad shifts in his seat. I know he fights calling me a liar.

I quickly say, "I came home to tell you and Lisa about my time with Jesus."

Then I add, "I need to review it for myself as much as share it with you."

"Good!" Lisa exclaims. "I've always imagined your adventure, and I can't wait to hear what it was like."

Dad nods with raised eyebrows and sits back.

"There's a lot to share," I warn. And I wonder, again, what they will think. How can I recount the profound experiences that have shaped me in the company of Jesus and left me rudderless now that he is dead?

Because I have committed myself to tell, I have to start somewhere. After a moment, I decide where to begin. I will start with the story they already know: Jesus's visit, two years ago. But I will share it from my perspective. I need to reveal what I felt and how I changed during that visit.

I tell them, for example, how proud I was to bring my hometown friends to the courthouse lawn and how I basked in Dad's pride of my association with a celebrated and famous person.

"I felt important that day," I share. "And I manipulated the event in order to put you up front before the bus pulled in. I made sure you and our friends could see and be seen."

Lisa smiles. "Of course!"

But I continue. "Yes, but what you don't know is something I'm not sure I can explain. It's something no one could observe but that I felt distinctly in my heart.

"It's that, one minute, I was riding high to be introducing everyone I knew to Jesus, and the next minute, I was drowning in guilt."

"Guilt?" my dad interrupts to ask.

"Yes. Guilt," I reply. "It hit me when I bypassed other needy people to pull you and my friends to the front of the waiting line.

What right do you have to do this? my conscience accused. *When was the last time you were so eager to bring others to Jesus? Why have you lacked the same compassion for the long lines of strangers who have thronged to Jesus every day in every town you have visited?*

"I was surprised by these thoughts. They jarred me and convicted me. And I saw myself and my role in Jesus's mission in a new light.

"I realized that no matter where we stopped or who came to us, Jesus never played favorites. Without fail, Jesus always lavished his care on the lowest of the low and the greatest of the great. No one was turned away.

"That conviction heightened my senses. Standing on the courthouse lawn I became aware of shadowed faces in the crowd— people I had not noticed before. Needy people. Hurting people. People I did not know. And I realized that as part of Jesus's inner circle, I had the power to promote or deny them access to him.

"And I responded to an overwhelming compulsion to leave you and my friends in your privileged spots at the front of the line and press my way into the crowd. One by one, I found and pulled other people forward. Into my line of friends, I inserted the neediest from the shadows. And, in their turn, Jesus touched and healed them all: my friends and my total strangers. And I was touched beyond anything I can express.

"You see, as Jesus healed those lines of people, he turned and looked at me. *Through* me, would better describe it; not *at* me. His look bored *into* me.

"Jesus's look told me he knew I had changed. His smile acknowledged that I, too, had received a healing: an unlocking of my heart and a new compassion to see people as he saw them.

"And with Jesus's eyes I began to see need everywhere!

"It seemed that every person we met had a need. In fact, everything seemed broken; everything groaned. I had a sense that the hard-packed earth groaned under our feet as we trampled it. I despaired that a sick tree had shed its leaves, that weeds choked an untended field, that a dead bird lay swarming with flies under its nest, that a hungry old man begged for pennies, that a child mourned a puppy hit by a car. The list was endless!

"With great difficulty, I made it through the day. I could not block out the burden Jesus felt. And I feel it, still, today.

"The next day on the bus when I observed Jesus sleeping in the back seat, I understood how drained he was. He had healed and taught from sunup to sundown in my hometown, just as he had everywhere we'd ever gone, every day.

"Everywhere we went, crowds of people made it impossible for Jesus to move. Even at night, strangers knocked on the doors of homes that had taken us in. On his way to worship—and even as he worshipped—people approached him or called out to him. Jesus was never free of the burden. Some of us tried to push the masses back, to give him breathing space. Sometimes we succeeded, but more often we did not.

"And even when Jesus was alone, he didn't sleep. Our group would awaken with the sun to find him returning from somewhere. We knew he hadn't slept but had gone to talk to the Father. And somehow, without sleep, he would meet the needs of the coming day.

"Only on the bus would it be quiet. Rides between towns were a blessing. When on the go, we rolled up the windows and turned off the cell phones. I, for one, seized those chances to nap.

"But our peaceful rides were not entirely free of challenges and dangers. One day, our bus ride nearly killed us."

Lisa's eyes widened.

"There must have been a slick spot or an oil spill on the pavement in the middle of a dark overpass because when the bus hit it at full speed we spun out of control. Terrified, Peter twisted the wheel and fought to avoid crashing through the guardrail. We grabbed our armrests and called out to God.

"Lost in exhaustion, Jesus slept until someone shook him awake. Half-conscious, he sat up. And just as the skid seemed to be winning and the guardrail was tenths of a second away, Jesus shouted a firm command.

"'Stop! Be still!'

"And, somehow—I'll never fathom how—we did not go over the side. The bus slid toward impact, and although it seemed destined to crash through the rail, it did not. Somehow the brakes held. Without a squeal or a jolt, we stopped as smoothly as if we had been approaching a red light on a quiet street in a school zone.

"Poor Peter still jerked the wheel, wild-eyed and hyper-ventilating, trying to save us. He didn't realize we had stopped. When his mind caught up and he looked around, Peter blinked and sat in a daze.

"The words 'Be still!' continued to ring in our ears, and, like Peter, I made myself breathe. My mind juggled the myriad impossibilities of our having cheated death.

"*What had happened? Had we just seen Jesus change the outcome of an impending accident? Or was I dreaming?*

"The hairs on my neck stood up, and my heart raced. What kind of man could defy the law of physics with a word? How had powers we could only guess at been engaged? How was it that our bus sat still and safe as if nothing unusual had happened? Time had stopped. And not even a jacket on the seat of the bus had fallen to the floor.

"Then reality resumed. Traffic approached, and we needed to move off the overpass.

"Jesus patted Peter's shoulder, and after expelling a *whew!* Peter put the bus into gear, and we moved.

"The effect of the miracle lingered, however, long after we reached our destination. We whispered about it, often. We also listened more intently when Jesus spoke and healed. His astounding display of power heightened our appreciation for his gifts, even his healing gift. We realized we had begun to take his healings for granted and treat them as commonplace. But in fact, Jesus's everyday healing power held no less miraculous weight than what we had experienced on the overpass.

"'You are the Christ, the son of the living God,' Peter confessed a short time later at a question from Jesus. And we agreed with Peter. But we had much to learn about what that declaration meant."

As I lean back on the sofa, Lisa still clasps her hands tightly. I am aware that my story is a lot for Dad and Lisa to swallow.

Dad's jaw is set. No doubt he thinks I'm crazy or at least a bit unhinged by my grief over Jesus's death. But neither he nor Lisa say anything. I am surprised, and I am glad. Dad would never have remained quiet, years ago. He has mellowed, and I sense he and Lisa are reserving judgment until I have finished.

It's good they do because the next part of my story is even more difficult to express to people who weren't there. How do I tell it?

I begin, "Not long after the overpass incident, Jesus took the twelve of us aside to coach us for the next step in our mentorship. Almost before we realized it, Jesus had sent us out to do what he had been doing."

Lisa asks, in surprise, "Do you mean, Jesus sent you out to heal and speak?"

I smile. Lisa is sharp.

"Yes, Lisa. That is what he expected us to do!"

I hurry, now, to resume my story before my dad can deny what I'm saying.

"It sounds preposterous," I admit, "but it happened."

"Jesus sent us out in pairs all over the region. And he gave us the power to heal people, just as he healed. And he charged us to tell everyone to repent of their sins and turn to God."

My dad interjects, "The nightly news didn't cover this!"

I press forward.

I say, "At first, we were as surprised as the people we served. But

God's power did flow through us, and we healed in Jesus's name. It was incredible!

"And in one town, when Philip and I were ministering, a stick-thin man came. He declared he had HIV and wasn't sure if we would help him. 'I'm a sinner,' he said, and he bowed low before us. As I looked at him, I recalled the many times Jesus had encountered others with HIV or similar diseases—diseases that produced fear and separation from society. And I remembered how Jesus always healed unconditionally and unreservedly. Jesus never shrank back. And so, I laid my hands on the man, and I called out for God's healing of his body, in Jesus's name.

"At once, color poured into his face, and muscle and flesh regenerated on his bones. After examining himself, the man fell to his knees. I told him to get up; that Philip and I were not the objects of his worship. Jesus was. And he went in search of Jesus, calling out his praise of Jesus to everyone he met."

Lisa whispers, "Praise God!" and I continue.

"Days later, when Philip and I returned with the others to report to Jesus on our ministries in his name, that man was in the crowd that never left Jesus's side. Mary Magdalene took him in."

So many hurting people, I reflect. *Without Jesus, they would have had no hope.*

"Jesus now kept the twelve of us with him," I say. "And people flocked to him from everywhere. The crowds were larger than ever. People came for so many reasons. Many came for healing. Some were gawkers caught up in the unique happenings. Others came just for Jesus's words. And no matter how late it got, those assembled refused to leave. They drank him in, like desert-starved wanderers.

"One crowd didn't disperse even when they ran out of food.

"And that is when Jesus fed them."

I chuckle as I share, "Somehow, Jesus multiplied the small lunch a boy had brought him. Jesus gave thanks for the lad's sandwiches, tore them apart, put the pieces into paper bags, and told us to hand out the bags. To this day, I don't understand how it happened, but the bits of food in those bags fed over 5,000 people!"

I hear Lisa clap her hands. "We caught a report of that on the news," she says. "Oh, how I wish I had been there! I would have loved it!"

I grin. "Yes, I can picture you there. You would have been urging seconds on everyone."

Dad grins, too, but he struggles with the miracle.

I continue. "Those who had eaten then sought to make Jesus their leader—perhaps, even, the country's leader. What a leader he would be! No one would ever be hungry or ill because Jesus could feed and heal them. Life would be perfect.

"Or so we thought.

"Strangely, the more Jesus's popularity grew the more he withdrew from it. It was odd. But as I look back, he must have known how things would end. We, on the other hand, were clueless, blinded by his miracles and the adulation of the crowds.

"Jesus disappeared more often to pray in secret. And he distanced himself from us by sending us ahead, alone, to our next destination. We tried to figure out how, at the last minute, he would show up. He always did. And one day we found out how he did it.

"That night, we needed to cover many miles, and Jesus insisted we leave him and drive on. We worried that this time he might not catch up.

"Because people had seen Jesus stay behind, the usual *groupie-convoy* was absent. In the quiet, Peter drove, and we dozed. The wind picked up as we crossed a bridge, and John suddenly pointed out something on the lake below.

"'It's Jesus!' John cried.

"Peter jammed on the brakes, and we peered into the darkness. Sure enough, below, on the lake, a figure walked on the waves.

"Nathanael's fingernails bit into my arm. 'Do you see this?' he whispered.

"James gasped, 'It's a ghost!'

"But John insisted, 'No! It's Jesus!'

"The figure called to us from the water. 'There's no need to fear; it's me,' we heard.

"And Peter shouted back, 'If it is you, Master, let me come down.'

"Jesus told Peter to come.

"Without hesitation, Peter stripped off his jacket and dove over the bridge rail."

"Oh, dear!" Lisa cries out.

I hurry to reassure her. "It wasn't far to the lake's surface, but the water was over a man's head and the waves were high. Peter bobbed for a moment, and then, somehow, he floated. From there, Peter rose to his knees and then his feet. And then, Peter walked to Jesus on the waves."

"Oh!" cries Lisa, again, at the wonder of it.

"We rubbed our eyes," I said. "But then, Peter faltered and sank. And Jesus had to pull him back to the wave tops. We were all riveted to the scene. And then Andrew ran to pull them up the bank as Jesus and Peter approached the shore.

"We stood, dumbfounded, until they reached us. And then, we joined Peter in falling to our knees in worship.

"We would still be bowed there, but Jesus said, 'We need to go.' He made us stand and board the bus."

I close my eyes, now, in an ache of remembrance and awe.

"We remained in a daze," I say, "but the miracle wasn't done, yet. Things kept happening.

"The minute Peter put the bus into gear, the bridge and the lake disappeared, and our destination, miles away, appeared in the bus headlights. We fell back in our seats in even more wonder."

Lisa now shakes her head. "Are you sure you weren't dreaming?"

I assure her all twelve of us recalled every detail of that night in the same way. There was no question it had happened.

I pause before I say, "Then, the next day, Jesus preached and healed. And as before, the crowds refused to leave. We ran out of food, and, again, Jesus fed us all."

My dad murmurs a quiet, "Amazing!" The way he says it warms me because it means he believes me. It encourages me as I continue.

"People everywhere talked of little, now, except that Jesus must be God's messiah.

"But aside from his miracles, Jesus didn't act like the messiah, the one who would unite the world. Instead, he began to talk about his *death*, and he seemed bent on making enemies. More than once, he stirred up the religious council at their headquarters. He denounced the leaders as vipers and thieves who took advantage of their role instead of drawing people to God."

"Yes," my dad says. "Those are the reports we heard in the news. We worried about you because Jesus was playing a dangerous game. We heard, twice, that when Jesus claimed to be God, the religious leaders rushed to kill him for blasphemy. But the news said he mysteriously escaped. Lisa and I wondered where you were during all of that. It was a relief to learn no one knew Jesus's whereabouts."

I say, "Yes, Jesus's brushes with the leadership unnerved us. We twelve had seen his power, and we were convinced he was the sent one of God. But the religious leaders had not seen those proofs. And instead of convincing them, Jesus alienated them.

"When Jesus set course for an isolated area once roamed by John, the baptizer, we celebrated. We wanted as much distance as possible between Jesus and the capital. We had worried about council tweets and posts asking for help to find Jesus. Here, it would be difficult for the authorities to penetrate the region and make an arrest. We felt secure.

"But our relief was short-lived. No sooner had we safely settled in our outpost than we received a text from Martha, one of Jesus's closest friends.

"'Our brother, your friend, is dying,' Martha wrote.

"Alarmed, we asked ourselves, why did this have to happen, now? We all knew it was a plea for Jesus to come back, and we assumed we would be turning around.

"We gassed up the bus and whispered among ourselves about the danger of returning. We hoped we could sweep in, heal Lazarus, and hurry out again.

"But Jesus surprised us. He made no move to board the bus. For days, we expected his signal to head out. Instead, he assured us that Lazarus's sickness would 'not end in death' but would 'give God glory and also glorify the son of God.'

"We were glad Lazarus would recover without us. It meant we didn't have to leave our haven.

"But a few days later, Jesus said Lazarus was dead and we were to drive to Martha's home.

"*What?* we wondered. *Why had Jesus let Lazarus die?*

"Jesus could have privately healed Lazarus and then raced back to safety. But now it was impossible to sneak in and out. Why flirt with danger to arrive late at a funeral?

"Going back in the middle of a crowded, public mourning would be suicidal. We reminded Jesus that the religious leaders were still out to kill him.

"But Jesus replied, 'There is time.'

"*What did that mean?* Time for what? Or more to the point, time *before* what? It sounded foreboding. Coupled with his earlier hints he would soon die, these were not reassuring words.

"Was Jesus not the messiah? Did Jesus's miracles mean nothing? Was Jesus just another prophet doomed to die? We could no longer ignore that possibility.

"And if so, where did that leave us? What should we do? We couldn't abandon him. Jesus had chosen us. We had been at the center of his remarkable ministry. How could we stay behind?

"I finally said out loud what the others were thinking: 'Let's go die with him.'

"So, with resignation and in loyalty to our master, we followed him onto the bus, and we went back.

"When we arrived, Martha cried, 'If you had been here Lazarus would not have died.' But she didn't condemn Jesus for his delay or deny his ongoing ministry. Instead, she said, 'Even now, I am certain that whatever you might ask of God, he will give you.'

"I admired Martha's allegiance to Jesus, even in the grip of her grief. And we listened as Jesus responded to her.

"Jesus answered Martha with a common word of comfort, that her brother would 'rise again.' Martha accepted his sympathy and returned the common response that, of course, 'Lazarus would rise again in the last day.'

"But then Jesus uttered a startling claim. He declared, 'I am the resurrection and the life; he that believes in me, though he were dead, will live. And whoever lives and believes in me will never die.'

"We wondered in amazement at the boldness of his words! Jesus was claiming himself to be the assurance, the reason, and the hope of rising again in the last day. We had heard Jesus speak often of the extreme righteousness needed in order to enter into eternal life. And, now, Jesus seemed to be saying he had the power to guarantee that life. What did he mean?

"Furthermore, Jesus made Martha say that she believed him! And she said it. She even said, in so many words, she believed anything Jesus might tell her because she knew he was the messiah, the son of God.

"We marveled at her faith. I prayed she was right and we were wrong. I prayed that Jesus's repeated predictions of his death would fail and he would assume his messianic role.

"Then Martha's sister, Mary, came and cried, also, that if Jesus had come earlier, Lazarus would not have died. And Jesus wept with her.

"Mary and Martha led us to the grave to pay our respects.

"A huge group of mourners trailed behind us, and the noise was considerable. Even Jesus groaned in grief.

"And then, Jesus stopped and turned to all of us.

"As we stood outside Lazarus's tomb of four days, Jesus commanded the mourners to roll the stone from the entrance. They hesitated, with good reason, because when they broke the seal on the tomb, the stench was unmistakable.

"Jesus stood his ground and called out loudly, 'Lazarus, come out of there!'

"I froze. Did Jesus expect us to believe…? And then, when I sensed movement from within the tomb, I feared Jesus was calling a ghost, or worse, a putrefying man to come out of that hole!

"And I drew back when a mummy-like figure stumbled into the light.

"Jesus, however, urged us forward. He commanded us to remove the grave clothes. And when we did, there stood a healthy, alive Lazarus! I trembled and sank to the ground."

As surprised as I had been to see Lazarus alive, I am not surprised when Dad interrupts me with the challenge, "So, where is that man, today?"

"He's living with his sisters," I say. "Swarms of people come to stare at him. And the authorities hate Lazarus because he is proof of Jesus's life-giving power from God."

Dad frowns. There were rumors but no news stories to corroborate the Lazarus event. But Dad doesn't interrupt again.

I continue. "As you can imagine, the raising of Lazarus refueled in his followers the call for Jesus to be their leader. Everyone expected him to assume his role soon. How could anyone resist a leader who could not only heal and feed people but also raise them from the dead? Such a leader would erase the fear of tragic shootings and bombings. Terrorism would lose its power. There would be no point to wars.

"Gone were my doubts about Jesus's messiahship.

"Instead, my companions and I dreamed of the high positions we might hold when Jesus came to power."

My dad frowns, now. He knows the end of the story, and he has already gone there. I plunge ahead, however.

"In the midst of all this," I say, "Jesus remained aloof. He retreated from the crowds and their intentions and repeated to us in private, 'I will be killed, soon.'

"*Why did he keep saying that?* It was unthinkable, now, that anyone would kill Jesus. He was too popular, 0and with his unique abilities,

Jesus could avoid any threat, just as he had changed the course of our bus on the overpass.

"Perhaps his words about his death weren't literal. He often spoke in parables we failed to grasp.

"But Jesus did not ascribe a lesson to these words. He just kept repeating them.

"Peter challenged him on it. But with a harshness I had never seen in Jesus, he rebuked Peter: Jesus even called Peter 'the devil!'

"Why did Jesus obsess about his *death* instead of his *messiahship*? Didn't he realize the possibilities? Didn't Jesus want people to honor him? Didn't he want to be their leader?

"And then, he changed. In a sudden, stunning reversal, Jesus roused the support of the people. At last, he not only accepted their acclaim, but he orchestrated a ticker-tape parade down the streets of the capital city."

I turned to Dad. "Did you watch the news coverage of Jesus riding high above the seats of a borrowed, dazzling, new convertible?"

I was surprised when Lisa shakes her head and Dad says it wasn't on the news. I can't believe it. I blurt out, "It should have been on the news! Thousands of people cheered Jesus, that day, and chanted slogans about him becoming the country's—maybe even the world's—leader.

"*This was more like it,* we twelve said to one another. *Things were coming together. It wouldn't be long, now, before Jesus would take up his position.*

"I rationalized that maybe Jesus's references to being *killed* were his way of saying the old life was going away and he was entering a new phase as the perfect ruler. I decided that must be it. It seemed to fit.

"But after the parade…" I paused to clear my throat.

"But after the parade," I began, again, "Jesus spoke more often of dying. And his voice carried great sorrow. He seemed intent on conveying a specific warning to us of impending disaster. But what were we supposed to do with this information? Were we supposed to protect him? If so, how?

"We were on a roller-coaster of, one minute, believing Jesus to be invincible and, the next, believing him capable of being killed. And we sometimes wondered if he was having a nervous breakdown. He was under tremendous pressure."

My throat tightens, now. I push forward. I have to finish my story.

"And then hell came," I say. "I call it *hell* because it is the only way to describe the events that took place a few days later. We watched in horror as armed officials led Jesus away. I say *watched*, but what I mean is we ran away, afraid we would be caught, too. It happened so fast. I'd like to say we surrounded and protected Jesus. But the truth is we didn't. And the worst of it was that Judas—one of our own circle— had betrayed him!

"The next few hours flew by with a rapidity no one could have foreseen. Peter tried to follow and help Jesus escape. But nothing Peter hoped for worked out. Instead, Peter stood by, helplessly, as long as he could. In trying to detract attention, Peter found himself denying even knowing Jesus, three times. When Peter realized what he had been doing, he broke down and left. He remained inconsolable for days.

"John is the one who saw, close up, Jesus cruelly beaten and then executed. Like Peter, John was unable to stop it. John even brought Jesus's mother in hopes of an appeal, but it was to no avail.

"The rest of us were so overcome with fear we remained in the shadows when he was dying. We cowered and wept. Everything was out of control. It was 'the overpass incident' all over again, except that this time our bus was plunging off the road. There was no stopping it.

"Our free fall had no bottom. Below us, only darkness loomed. We were certain it would swallow us up. We talked about where to flee until things cooled off.

"Two men from our larger company, with political access, gained permission to take Jesus's body for burial. At least Jesus would be buried and not continue to hang exposed like many criminals did. We couldn't have borne it.

"Some of us, who were well-disguised, followed Jesus's torn and lifeless body to the tomb.

"And then…" I have to swallow.

"And then," I say," the stone was rolled into place.

"All hope was lost, and I left to come home."

Now, I sit. In the presence of my father, I refuse to wallow in my grief. Only Lisa's eyes fill with tears.

Part Two

With the passing of Mom and the moving out of my brothers and sisters, the notorious table talk of our supper hour has lapsed into history. Lisa has made a small attempt at conversation, but neither Dad nor I have much to say. Dad did express doubts about parts of my story, but he seems to accept much of what I've shared. And now that I have told my story, I have begun to analyze why I have come here.

What had I expected to find? How did I think I could come back? Everything has changed. I am no longer the boy who played here; and the man I've become no longer fits within my dad's walls.

But I don't belong in my other world, either—the starry-eyed world of the popular religious figure to whom I had entrusted my future. Jesus has left me orphaned.

Where am I to go? What am I to do?

A long walk after supper does nothing to settle my profound sense of loss.

An explosion of knocking jolts the household awake early in the morning. My irritated dad yanks open the front door to find our neighbor, Max McGuire, dancing on the porch in his bathrobe and bare feet.

"Have you seen the news?" Max cries. "What does Thomas think? I saw him walking last night, so I know he's home."

Lisa turns on the kitchen television and starts a pot of coffee.

"Sit," Dad says.

No matter which station we turn to, the news is the same: "The disciples of Jesus have stolen his body. What you are seeing is his empty tomb."

"No!" I exclaim. "That's not true. No one could have slipped past the council guards to steal anything."

Despite my denials, various council officials take the microphone to express their outrage at the theft. "These Jesus rabble-rousers don't understand who they're up against," they spit.

A surge of anger rises in me. The only rabble-rousers are the religious officials!

Max turns to catch my reaction.

"What a bunch of hooey," I say. "It's a setup. I'll bet the council removed Jesus's body, themselves, to discourage pilgrimages. Jesus helped thousands of people who would come to honor him."

Then I add, "Why would we steal his body? It wouldn't serve any purpose for us. Jesus is dead, and that's the end of everything."

I no sooner finish my defense when another official says, "We think they stole the body because Jesus said 'destroy this temple, and I will raise it again in three days.' Some have interpreted those words as Jesus's way of saying he would raise his body from the dead in three days."

I shake my head, and the interviewer smirks. "Isn't that claim preposterous?" he asks. "When you're dead, you're dead, right?"

The council official frowns when someone from the crowd shouts: "Jesus raised Lazarus from the dead. If Jesus could do that, couldn't he raise himself from the dead?"

"Hearsay!" the official scoffs. "Who would buy that story? Jesus is dead. I witnessed his execution with my own eyes. There was no fakery involved. And I can assure you the blasphemer is in hell, right now. There's no coming back!"

Again, I flush with anger.

The news reporter faces the camera and assumes a serious air. He says, "We've been following this story since early this morning when three women who visited the tomb claimed they saw Jesus alive. As preposterous as it sounds, here is that interview."

I sit up. There are Mary Magdalene, Joanna, and Mary the mother of James. And I marvel at their excitement. What a change from the grieving mourners I left!

I observe, too, how bright and pleasant the tomb garden looks in the early morning light—a marked difference from the sinister blackness that shrouded everything when Jesus was put into the grave.

"Yes, Jesus is alive!" says Joanna. (I moan, in spite of myself.) "We expected to have to beg for access to the tomb this morning to finish treating his body. But when we got there, we found no guards, and the tomb was open. Inside, we found empty grave clothes. Jesus was not there."

The reporter interrupts to clarify: "You're saying there was no body, but Jesus's grave clothes were there—so, somebody took their time in removing him from the tomb?"

Mary Magdalene answers, "It wasn't *somebody* moving him. It was Jesus, himself. He's alive! He talked with me."

The clip ends, and the reporter sums up for his news audience: "I'll leave you to decide whom you believe—a bunch of hallucinating women or the authorities in charge of the tomb. Either way, it's been an eventful morning. We hope to have more for you in the hours ahead. For now, I'm Ron Strong, reporting from outside an empty grave that held Jesus's body, three days ago."

Max turns. "Do you know those women?" he asks. "Are they touched in the head?"

The question unsettles me and takes me back to when I first saw Mary Magdalene.

Jesus saw her, first. He edged his way through a
crowd to where Mary sat, a crumpled and insignificant

physical, mental, and moral mess. I overheard a man nearby repeat a salacious tidbit about her and label her as demon-possessed.

When Jesus reached Mary and spoke, she blinked and turned to look at him. Their eyes met, and Mary's mouth fell open in surprise. Jesus reached out to help her stand, and for a moment, Mary stood with her face averted.

An awful voice rose from her throat. 'Go away!' it growled, and my skin crawled at the sound of it. Jesus stood firm, however, and more voices rose from within Mary—several voices at once, in a whole chorus of threats. 'Go away!' they demanded. 'Leave us alone!'

The pitiful prettiness of Mary's face contorted into an ugly mask. But her eyes held a pathetic plea.

Jesus bowed in prayer. Then he laid his hand upon her head and commanded, 'Come out of this woman! Leave her, now!'

I watched as Mary's body twisted and a host of violent screams tore around us. Jesus held fast. And after a moment, the air grew still. Mary clung to Jesus like a drained soul.

When she finally looked up, I gasped. She was beautiful! Her eyes were clear, and a lilting laughter floated from her lips. She was not the same woman I had seen earlier, heaped like garbage on the ground at the edge of the crowd.

When Jesus released her, Mary danced away to music she, alone, heard. A short time later, she returned bringing others, and they all praised God and thanked Jesus. After that, Mary appeared many times in the crowds in various towns we visited. She found it impossible to stay away.

That is what I remembered about Mary. Crazy? Yes, Mary had once been crazy. But now…

"Yes, these women are friends," I tell Max. "I'm sure they believe what they think they saw."

I sigh. I imagine that part of the women's story comes from a wishful hope. I am less concerned about their interpretation of events than that the authorities might persecute them.

My cell phone suddenly vibrates, and a message lights up the screen: "Come back, Thomas! He's here! You're missing out!"

I flinch at the message and its timing. *What? Is Matthew suffering delusions, too?* I have never known Matthew to let his emotions sway him from hard facts. Neither Nathanael nor Matthew deal in grays.

For the benefit of those in the kitchen, I tear my eyes from the phone and shrug off my frown. "Just a message confirming the other ten are safe," I say.

"So," insists Max, again, "what does it all mean? Did your friends take Jesus's body? Were you in on it?"

Then he adds in a conspiratorial whisper, "Is that why you're hiding out, here?"

"No. On all counts," I declare firmly. "I came home to visit."

Lisa changes the topic, and we finish our coffee and some breakfast rolls. She catches me up on how the townspeople Jesus healed are doing, today. And Max slaps my back with, "Your Jesus was just what this town needed!"

I wince. *My Jesus* isn't here anymore.

Eventually Max leaves, and I retreat to my room. I want no more company or speculation. I need to think, to decide what to do and where to go from here. What does the follower of a dead prophet do?

Dead *prophet*. Even as I say the words to myself, I reject them.

Jesus was more than a mere prophet. I had once accepted him as the messiah. But it made no sense for the messiah to die!

For several nights, I sleep little. While the household lies quiet, my thoughts clamor for resolution. What am I going to do? Where should I be? What would Jesus have wanted me to do? Even if he is dead, I can still honor him, can't I?

Then one morning, I lay the issue to rest.

I will return to the others. I belong with those who have walked with Jesus and been part of his ministry. Ours is a unique brotherhood. Together, we can keep his memory and teachings alive. And if the authorities pursue and kill us, I am ready to die.

My decision isn't easy for my dad. He worries for my safety and wants me to stay.

But when I insist, Dad is the one who drives me to the capital. He drops me off near the last place I met with my companions and Jesus before his death.

"I hope you know what you're doing," Dad says. His grip is fierce and his hug long when he says goodbye. I wave and watch until the car turns out of sight.

I wonder if I will see Dad and Lisa, again. But I suffer no regrets. I am convinced this is where I belong.

The second-floor windows of the big stone house before me look in on a large upper room where our group ate our final meal together. I knock and wait. After a flutter at the curtain, the owner answers. I ask if he knows where the others might be. He doesn't know, and he seems frightened. I thank him, descend from the porch, and walk on.

I pull out my phone and reply to Matthew's text: "I'm here; where are you?" Seconds after I hit *Send*, Matthew's answer comes: "Someone will meet you at the coffee shop corner."

"Fine," I reply, and I make my way to the familiar spot.

When I arrive, I pay for a coffee and take it to a table under an umbrella to wait.

Before I have drained my bold brew, I spy Philip. Philip waves and hurries across the street. When he reaches and greets me, he whispers, "Welcome back!"

Then Philip says, "Come on," and I toss my half-empty cup into the trash. I follow Philip silently down several side streets and alleys. Through a dark doorway, we enter a tall apartment building and take the elevator to the top floor. The corridor window overlooks the city skyline. But Philip doesn't linger. He hurries me down the hall and knocks on a door. From the rustle inside, I guess someone is checking through the peephole before answering.

When the door flies open, Matthew pulls me into the room. "I'm glad you've come!" he exclaims. "So much has happened!"

My companions, and others I recognize, gather around and talk over one another in their excitement at seeing me. I laugh at their welcome.

"Whoa!" I protest. "I can't listen to all of you, at once."

Matthew shushes them and says, "He's alive, Thomas!" The others bob their heads.

I grimace. "I watched the interview of the women saying the same thing."

Matthew laughs. "Sounds crazy, doesn't it?" he says. "You can imagine our derision when the women returned from the tomb on Sunday morning with news that an angel told them Jesus was alive. And Mary Magdalene insisted she had met and talked with Jesus!

"We scoffed. We had seen Jesus's body and noted the great stone and grave seal set in place. No one could have moved that stone behind the backs of the council guards. And, let's face it, nobody comes back from the dead."

"Right," I affirm solidly.

"But," says Matthew, "one look at Lazarus in our midst told us otherwise. Death is not final. The impossible might be possible."

I frown. *Yes, Jesus had raised Lazarus, but no one has ever raised themselves.*

Matthew says, "Peter and John took off to verify the women's story. And they, too, found the empty grave clothes in an open tomb."

I shake my head. *Did someone steal the body?*

But Matthew now says, "Thomas, the best part came Sunday night. We had just eaten the evening meal when we noticed a man at the end of the table."

Matthew points to the spot. He says, "At first, I imagined he was one of us. But then, I realized he was a stranger—someone who had broken in. But how? The door was bolted fast. We never leave it open; it is too dangerous.

"And when I looked again, I recognized him! It couldn't be, but it was. Jesus was alive and right here with us!"

The others ratify Matthew's claim with a chorus of *yeses.*

I step back. But Matthew closes up the gap between us.

"Oh, Thomas!" Matthew exclaims in my face, "Jesus scolded us for not accepting the women's reports. But then he pronounced 'Peace' over us. It took several minutes for us to get past the shock. We had to get our minds around what our eyes were seeing. And Jesus took care to prove he was not a ghost or phantom.

"We hugged him and felt his hugs back. And we cried to have the Teacher teaching us, again!"

Everyone murmurs their confirmation of Matthew's story.

I turn away. This makes no sense. *If Jesus came here, where is he?*

But Matthew continues, "Jesus charged us to tell our friends we had seen him.

"And then," says Matthew, "he left, as mysteriously as he had come!"

"He left?" I say. "What does that mean?"

Matthew says, "It just means he left. And we've been trying to make plans all week. It isn't safe to leave here, yet, but we want the others to have the news."

The excitement in Matthew's eyes blazes in the eyes of the others.

I see it and want to believe, but it's too unbelievable. *What has possessed these men to believe this impossible story?*

Matthew smiles. "I wouldn't have believed it, either, if I hadn't seen Jesus, myself."

"Yeah," I say. "This is too much to accept on the word of someone else—even you. I barely get my mind around the raising of Lazarus, which I witnessed. And you're saying Jesus has raised himself from the dead. Not even the miracle-working prophet Elisha did that! Besides, Jesus's execution left him torn and twisted in ways Lazarus never was. If Jesus were raised, he would still have that scarred body, wouldn't he?"

Matthew nods. "Jesus does still bear the wounds. But he's different, Thomas. I can't explain it."

I sigh. "You can't explain it, and I can't believe it. I can't believe Jesus is alive. If he is, he would be here, wouldn't he? And I would be able to see him and put my fingers in the nail holes of his hands and my hand into his speared side."

I hurry to say, "I'm ready to defend Jesus's memory and carry on his teachings, but it'll take another miracle for me to accept that he's alive."

The room brightens as the words leave my mouth. I assume the sun is setting and shining in the window.

"Jesus!" someone whispers.

In surprise, I look up. And I stare.

Jesus stands before me. Or is it my imagination?

I look away and then back again.

He is still there.

I pull in a deep breath and whisper, "Is it you?"

I grip the edge of the table. My mind whirls with a million thoughts and then settles on the one I had last expressed: my doubt.

I bury my face. But Jesus lifts my chin. I tremble at his touch.

And Jesus says, "Here. Put your fingers here, Thomas, in the nail holes in my hands."

Through my tears, I let him guide my fingers. The piercings I had mourned so deeply when they had happened are there, but Jesus no longer flinches in pain.

"Now," Jesus urges, "put your hand in the wound in my side."

I can't pick up my hand. It hangs limply. But through my tears I see the ugly, open wound where a soldier's spear has thrust upward, tearing Jesus's flesh and sending blood and water spraying to the ground.

Jesus smiles, the way one smiles to reassure a small child. "Stop doubting," he says. "Stop doubting and believe."

My legs crumble. I fall at his feet, and I cry, "My Lord! My Lord, and my God!"

Over the next month, those of us in the apartment building move away from the city and closer to home. I visit Dad and Lisa and tell them all that is happening. My dad surprises me by believing my story. The change he sees in me cannot be denied!

Jesus surprises some of us at the seashore, where he reaffirms Peter. And then later, when we all gather again, Jesus appears often and teaches us many things. In joy, I hang on his every word. He prepares us for all that is to come. We will remain behind, one more time.

We are saddened at his leaving. But we accept it, without protest. (Peter pulls no guns this time, as he did during the arrest in the Garden.)

We understand that his leaving is to return *home*. Jesus belongs in the other world. He is going ahead, to prepare our places for when our work, in his name, will end. We will join him in our time.

On the day of his departure, I rejoice that I no longer doubt things beyond my understanding. With the others, I watch Jesus rise into the clouds. No planes or helicopters or jetpacks, just the power of God lifting his son slowly back into his presence.

As Jesus disappears, his words remain: "Don't stand there; it's time to go. Carry on my business. Tell people who the Father is and who I am. Call them to repentance and belief in my salvation. Baptize them in the name of the Father, the Holy Spirit, and me. Teach people to do everything I have taught you. And don't worry; even though I'm leaving you, you will not be alone. I will send my spirit to you, soon, to help you."

Two angels appear, who tell us, "Jesus will return in a similar way, one day," and that image undergirds me in the face of the difficulties of this world.

When we return to the capital, as Jesus has instructed, we receive his gift: the Holy Spirit. I am no longer alone. And now, I not only *see* with Jesus's eyes but I also *hear* and *feel* in new ways. Scripture leaps from the pages and fills my thoughts and heart. And I am compelled to witness to every person I meet, for the rest of my life.

With the others, I minister his love, his saving grace, his hope, and his promises. And we reach more people than Jesus ever could have in his flesh.

While we work, we watch for his returning in the clouds and long for his new heaven and new earth. For then, his transforming touch on the world will be complete.

Even so, Lord Jesus, come!

2

VISIONS

As we watched, the police boat on the sea grew from a mere speck on the horizon to a shimmering silhouette and then a puttering reality that revealed three people on board. John was coming home.

For years, only John's occasional letters and manuscripts had confirmed he still lived. And when Anna and I received word of his release from prison, we raced to meet him.

How John had survived Patmos was a miracle. He had already been white-haired when whisked away to work in the island's penal mines. His crime? Worshipping the risen Jesus.

Anna gripped my arm as John's frail figure was carried to shore. "We were right to bring the wheelchair," she whispered.

It seemed an eternity until the required paperwork was completed and the police beckoned us. We hurried forward.

John's face glowed at the sound of our voices, but his eyes had dimmed and did not track our movements.

"Benny! Anna!" he cried, and we squeezed him with our welcoming hugs.

"We have a room all set for you," said Anna. "And a good supper."

"Ah!" John exclaimed. "A good supper! I have almost forgotten how real food tastes!"

On the drive home, we repeated things about ourselves and our family that we'd already written him in letters.

"Did anyone read our letters to you?" Anna asked.

John assured us that a fellow-prisoner had not only read to him but had also put John's words on paper for us.

"Levi was very helpful," John said. "I was thankful for him. Perhaps you remember Levi? You would recall him from your childhood days. Levi and his friends were always at Jesus's feet or engaging him in games."

Anna nodded. "I do remember Levi! Is he well? Will he be released, soon, too?"

John gently replied, "Levi died of malaria a couple of months ago."

The deaths of our friends was nothing new. Many had been imprisoned and killed. And none of John's colleagues had survived. The brutal persecution that had followed Jesus's death had exacted a great toll.

"There are so many in paradise," I observed quietly.

"Yes. And yet, somehow, I have survived," John said.

After we settled John into a comfortable living room chair, Anna cleared the supper table. John and I dozed. It had been a long and emotional day.

With my eyes closed, I reflected on my earliest memories of John.

> As a close associate of the healer named Jesus, John was a regular customer of my parents' business, and he would tease me while waiting for his food.
>
> Mom and Dad fed people. My parents traveled and set up shop wherever Jesus's bus stopped. Back in town at our little family-owned eatery, a sign hung on the door that read, "Closed Until Further Notice." It hung there for over two years. During that time, I remember visiting every ball field and fairground where Jesus spoke. The sides of our large camper hooked open so the crowds who gathered could order hot or cold sandwiches and sodas from the window. John came every day with an order for Jesus and the twelve of Jesus's closest associates.

My parents were not alone in capitalizing on the crowds that thronged after the healer. Other merchants sold ice cream, hot pretzels, clothing, sunglasses, or sunbrellas. Business held brisk—until Jesus emerged from his bus. That was the signal to close up shop and rush to hear him speak.

When Jesus's twelve bodyguards emerged to set up a perimeter, word flew, and our customers disappeared. The masses jockeyed to stake out a spot as close to the front as possible. No one wanted to miss a word or be too far away to see the healings.

Only shouts of "Make way! We have a sick person, here!" swayed listeners to yield access to the front. Otherwise, no one budged from their position.

The sick and disabled formed the first row of the audience to await a touch from Jesus after he finished speaking. The rest of the crowd craned their necks to watch those touches.

Even I had seen a healing.

From my dad's shoulders I had seen Jesus heal my little neighbor. Anna had battled cancer from the age of three. Her family and friends had hovered and watched as she had approached death by inches.

"Don't bring Anna out in the crowds," well-meaning people warned, but her parents insisted they were bringing her to Jesus, in spite of the dangers. The naysayers predicted, "She's too fragile, and she'll get an infection."

But Mr. and Mrs. Woodrum had not listened. They had believed in Jesus's power, and they had brought Anna to him. And I had watched her pale cheeks bloom and her limbs flesh out as Jesus healed her.

Jesus not only saved Anna, but he gave Anna and me a future. If Anna had died sixty-five years ago, we would *not have married and produced three children and eight grandchildren.*

After Anna's healing, the Woodrums joined the Jesus-caravan. And Anna and I played among a host of children who grew up hearing Jesus speak and marveling at his miracles.

I was only eight when I observed my first non-healing miracle. And it involved me.

After an unusually long day of travel, the Jesus-bus stopped at an isolated campground. In an attempt to keep up with the caravan, my parents and other merchants had not restocked their goods and food supplies along the way. So, we were out of everything. And there were no area restaurants or fast-food places to take up the slack.

Even if there had been places nearby, few people would have left the camp and risked losing their parking spots. They would rather wait for the vendors to restock and reopen tomorrow than be stuck on the outer edges of the grounds.

Jesus didn't wait, however. He started to teach the minute the bus wheels stopped. Everyone, including my family, scrambled to hear.

Mom and Dad listened as long as they could, but when suppertime approached, they prepared to drive some distance away to pick up supplies. (Dad had called ahead.) It would be a long night for us, but people needed food to eat, tomorrow, and this was our business. I helped fold up things so we could leave.

Then, before we left, my dad said, "Here. This is for you."

Puzzled, I opened a bag to find two small fish sandwiches and some extra buns. "I don't want you to go hungry, tonight," Dad said.

My tummy rumbled in anticipation, and, at first, I was excited for the food. But then, because I saw only one bag, I asked, "Where are your sandwiches?"

My mother said, "Your father and I will eat in the morning, son. These are for you."

I protested. How could I eat when my parents were hungry? I knew how hard they worked, and although I was hungry, I felt guilty.

When I said so, my dad chuckled. "Mama," he said, "our boy is growing up."

My mother smiled, and I stood a little taller.

I declared, again, "I can't eat these sandwiches unless you have something to eat, too."

And then, an idea came to me. I said, "Why don't we give these sandwiches to Jesus? He must be hungry. He's traveled, too, and taught all day, and he needs his strength for tomorrow. Couldn't I take them to him?"

My dad looked surprised, and he nodded his approval. Then, as I had seen him do so often in my life, he lifted his eyes to heaven. "Thank you, God, for a good son. As Benny suggests, we are offering this small meal for your servant. May you bless it to him."

Then my father opened the camper door, and I stepped down with my package. I was being sent, alone, to see Jesus. I advanced proudly, bearing my precious gift in both hands drawn close to my chest.

I felt very grown up to be entrusted with this special mission. But as I advanced through the maze of vehicles, I was glad I was small and able to slip between the cracks in the crowd. And just as I reached Jesus's bus, Jesus finished speaking and healing.

Because I couldn't find John, I gave my bag to Andrew, another of Jesus's band.

I lingered, wondering if I would hear Jesus's appreciation when Andrew gave him my sandwiches. But instead, I overheard Jesus tell his men to "feed the crowd."

It surprised me. Did Jesus have food we didn't know about? Had I wasted my supper?

That thought dissolved when I heard Jesus's men protest. Not only could they not cover the cost, but there was nowhere to buy even a small amount of food.

I was just a kid but I wondered why Jesus had given such an outlandish order.

Then, I heard the crinkle of a paper bag, and I saw Andrew thrust my sack at Jesus. As if to illustrate the unreasonableness of Jesus's command, Andrew said, "All we have is a sack lunch this lad has sent for you. That's all! There's nothing available to feed anyone else."

I expected Jesus to say a thank you to take back to my parents. But instead, he opened my bag, pulled out the sandwiches, separated them into bite-sized pieces, and distributed the pieces among several paper bags. Then, he ordered the crowd to arrange themselves in small groups on the grass. He offered a prayer of thanks and instructed his men to distribute the bags.

As I watched in wonder, the paper bags never seemed to grow empty. How could this be?

Remarkably, after everyone in the crowd had eaten their fill, there were twelve filled bags left over. I was glad there was enough remaining for Jesus and his disciples. I couldn't wait to tell my parents what I had seen.

I turned to leave, but John stopped me. He and Andrew stooped down and said, "Thank your parents, lad."

And then, Andrew handed me two bags and patted my head.

*Wow! My tennis shoes barely touched the ground
as I raced to our camper. We, too, would eat our fill of
miracle food for supper.*

No one went hungry.

After rousing briefly, John's eyes had closed, again. Anna and I smiled and watched his cheeks puff to the rhythm of a light snore. He had begun a reminiscence but had dropped off in the middle of a sentence.

Then, like the toy rabbit in a battery commercial, John's eyes flew open. He realized where he was, and he apologized for sleeping.

Stroking his beard, he asked, "Where was I?"

I said, "You had just told us that Jairus, one of the local religious leaders, had asked Jesus to come and heal his dying daughter. And you said Jesus stopped to heal another woman before getting into Jairus' car."

"Ah, yes," John said. "The woman's healing delayed Jesus. And then a text came bearing bad news. Jairus's child had died, and she no longer needed healing.

Then John said, "Jesus seldom moved quickly, as you know, but now he suddenly whirled about, and before Jairus could react or shed a tear over the awful news, Jesus drew within inches of his face. Staring into Jairus's eyes, Jesus said, 'Don't be afraid; only believe.'

"The astonished Jairus held Jesus's gaze and nodded slowly. Then, Jesus motioned for me, James, and Peter to accompany him, and we set off in Jairus's car.

"When we arrived, we could hear the girl's mother and others weeping. The mother flung herself on her husband's chest when he reached her.

"And above the noise of the mourning, Jesus announced loudly and calmly that the girl was not dead but only sleeping. We were surprised, to say the least. And many mourners snarled and leaped from their chairs. *Who was this cruel person?*

"Peter, James, and I rushed to surround Jesus, and we moved into the girl's room. Jairus motioned for the others to stay back. He took his wife's hand and led her into the room with us. Then he shut the bedroom door.

"Jairus comforted his wife at their daughter's bedside, and Jesus brushed past them. Jesus sought the girl's pale hand and after the briefest of prayers, he said, 'Child, you can get up, now.'

Our astonished minds were still taking in his command when a cool draft, like a breath, entered the room. James, Peter, and I gasped as the child's chest rose. Then she yawned and opened her eyes. With a stretch of her arms, the girl sat up. Her feet slipped to the floor, and she stood on tip-toes to gather hugs from her mother and father.

"Although we had witnessed hundreds of healings, James, Peter, and I stood speechless.

"Before Jairus's wife could faint away, Jesus caught her attention. He suggested, 'I believe your daughter needs something to eat.' His words rallied the woman, and she cried, 'Of course! Of course! I'll get something, right away.'

"She crossed the room, but Jesus stalled her. 'Tell no one,' he said. She looked surprised. But then she understood. We all understood. No one wanted the girl to become a gazing stock.

'She was just in a coma,' Jairus suggested to his wife. 'She was just asleep.'

The woman smiled and said, 'I understand, my husband.' But her grateful eyes spoke the truth all of us in the room knew."

John sat back, now, and closed his eyes. It gave me a moment to replay the story. *What if that had been my little girl?* I mused. *I wouldn't have been able to contain myself!*

The storyteller's eyes remained closed, and I wondered if we should rouse him, this time, for bed. But John again surprised us and sat forward with a smile.

He said, "It messes with your mind when someone you know can bring people back from the dead. And Jesus did it again: he raised a widow's son at Nain, and he raised Lazarus from the grave.

"You were just children," John said, "but I'm sure you noticed when people began to clamor for Jesus to lead a military revolt to free us from the forces occupying our country. If Jesus could revive dead soldiers, victory would be assured. That's what a messiah could do!"

John was right. I remember the rallying cries and shouted slogans. And I knew the stories of the promised messiah.

"Jesus had other powers, as well," John said. "We can talk about those, tomorrow. For now, it's enough to say that the twelve of us who traveled with him fell under the messiah dream, too. My brother James and I were bold enough to ask for privileged positions when Jesus came into power. We had no idea what we were asking, of course. We simply heard Jesus insisting we were his *friends*. I laugh, now, because we had no idea what it meant to be *friends* with Jesus.

"In spite of all the time we had spent with him, we still had no concept of who Jesus truly was. We had seen miracle after miracle and had confessed him to be the *son of God*, but the full truth of that term had eluded us. We viewed our miraculous teacher as a great man sent *from God* but had not made the leap to identify him *as God!* I recall, now, all the times Jesus told and showed us his godhead, but we were too earthly-minded to take it in.

"One event in particular should have opened our eyes, but even that failed to drive home the indisputable truth to our dull senses.

"The revelation came when Jesus took Peter, James, and me in a rented car up a steep mountain pass. We arrived at what felt like the top of the world. We filled our lungs, and Jesus walked ahead a short distance.

"Then, without warning, Jesus began to change.

"I can only describe it by saying that everything about him, even his blue-jeans and T-shirt, radiated a white light painful to look at. Through shielded eyes we observed two bright figures with him: Elijah and Moses. (Don't ask how we knew who they were; we just did.) James, Peter, and I stood outside their circle, but we could see in as the shining three talked. We knew we were observing a quantum leap into an alternate spiritual dimension. And this was no movie or television program. This was real!

"Peter tried to speak in the middle of the vision, to offer a proper response, but a voice from heaven interrupted and said, 'This is my beloved son; listen to him.' And immediately, Moses and Elijah disappeared. Once again, Jesus and the three of us stood alone in the middle of the road at the top of the mountain.

"Jesus calmly climbed into the car, and in a daze, we got in, too. James took the wheel, and we started down. The only words spoken were from Jesus. He said we were not to tell anyone what we had seen, 'until the son of man has risen from the dead.' His words burned in us, but what did 'until the son of man has risen from the dead' mean?

"Of course, we now know exactly what it means. But, at the time, we could not foresee his death, burial, and resurrection—all the things that have now brought the meaning of Jesus's life into full focus."

Now, John turned to me. Perhaps he was tired of talking, because he asked me, "What do you remember of Jesus's last days?"

I thought for a moment and said, "Confusion, mostly. I was still a child, and I couldn't grasp what was happening. What comes to mind, first, is the parade into the capital."

Anna murmured, "Yes, I remember that, too."

I relived that day for him, as the memories came.

"Hosanna! God save us!" I cheered and shouted with my parents and thousands of other celebrants along the parade route. We had come to the capital for the annual religious festival, and we thrilled to see Jesus honored on his approach to the city. Like others, I believed this display confirmed that Jesus was the messiah. My parents had said so.

I expected the authorities to meet and honor Jesus at the city gates. But they weren't there. Perhaps their reception would happen in the council headquarters, and we would see coverage on the news when we got back to our hotel room.

But nothing appeared in the news about the parade or the welcome of the messiah. I remember asking why, and my parents didn't know. I heard them discussing it with friends, but because of my age, I wasn't allowed to join their conversation. I only knew they sensed trouble.

The next time I saw Jesus, days later, from our hotel window above the street, I barely recognized him. Jesus was bloodied and bent in pain under the weight of a huge wooden cross. Stunned, I wondered, Why? What had brought this about?

My parents mumbled something about an unusual public execution, and they shielded me from the full horror of it. I did hear that one of Jesus's inner circle had betrayed him and had set in motion his arrest and death sentence. Surely, it wasn't John, I thought. I wouldn't want to believe that of John.

The next morning, I learned Jesus was dead.

I wept. Why had they killed him? I still naively believed that only evil people were executed. Not good people. And Jesus was good.

Even worse to my young mind, the festival continued as if his death had not happened.

It seemed wrong to me that nothing could stop tradition. With all those who had come to the capital, my family observed the required customs. And I cried through it all.

After the observance ended, we returned home, to a place I barely knew. I remained glum and was surprised that my parents didn't chastise me for it.

My dad took down the "Closed Until Further Notice" sign from the window of our eatery, and we tried to resume our old life. But although former customers returned, our sense of purpose did not. Nothing, now, seemed truly alive. Life had gone to a grave, and memories had been reduced to whispers. Would our lives be this way forever?

And then, something changed.

On our fourth morning back in town, my dad burst into the eatery kitchen with breathless news that Jesus had been seen alive! Mom and I stared in amazement. Dad had never been one to trade in rumors, and this one was beyond far-fetched.

Others came whispering the same news—whispering because the authorities who had put Jesus to death were also bent on putting the rumors of him to death.

Arrests filled the news. Council authorities were rounding up close associates of Jesus. Would we be imprisoned, too?

Anna and I listened as our parents talked late into the night. We remained wide-eyed when, in the wee hours, they moved our food camper and a great stock of supplies to a secluded field far outside the city. I'm sure you remember the spot that belonged to farmer Kessler, a secret follower of Jesus. Our vehicle joined dozens of cars and campers taking shelter in the valley between three wooded hills.

You, John, and Peter and Andrew visited, one day, and insisted you had seen the risen Jesus and had talked with him. We tried to imagine Jesus alive and dreamed of seeing him, too.

Peter declared, "Jesus told us to trust in him and not be afraid. He wants us to spread the news. And he has promised he will always be with us."

No sooner had Peter said these words than a gasp went up from several in our group. I stretched to see what

those who were taller were seeing. And there he was!
Jesus had appeared!

John laughed with joyous happiness at my remembrance. "Yes!" he said. "Jesus appeared and taught us all we needed to know. And when he finally left and sent his holy spirit, I recall that you, my young friend, were anointed, too!"

"Yes!" I exclaimed. "I hadn't expected it, because I was not yet a man, but its fire fell on me, just the same."

"And me, too!" Anna cried.

I squeezed Anna's hand, and I said, "Immediately, like our parents and our friends, we grew bold. We shared all we had seen and heard. And the spirit remained with us as Anna and I grew up.

"And then, John, you were banished to your island prison where we feared you would die. But even as the rest of the disciples suffered martyrdom, you survived and lived on. And here you are!"

It was dark, now, and John's hair glistened like snow in the lamplight. I asked, "Do you want to continue this, tomorrow?"

John sat forward and put his hands on his knees. "No!" he said emphatically. "I don't want to go to bed until I've shared how the visions changed me."

I sat forward, now. Although Anna and I had read John's widely published *Revelation*, I wanted to hear about the visions, first hand.

John's eyes glowed with passion as he spoke.

"As you know," he said, "the visions came to me on worship day— the one day of the week we prisoners were allowed to rest.

"I had prayed, as I normally did. And, as I was in the spirit, I heard a mighty voice, like a trumpet sounding. And the voice instructed me to write down the things I was about to see.

"I turned to face the speaker, expecting to see an angel. But my knees gave out when, instead, I saw Jesus.

"And the Jesus I saw was more awesome and fearfully powerful than any angel I had ever imagined. I was humbled to dust by my unworthiness to be in his presence. My mind could barely take in the risen Christ in his full glory as the son of God.

"There I was, John, who had been a devoted disciple and who had seen Jesus transfigured and shining on a mountain top and who had seen the risen Jesus when he had appeared shortly after his death, and, yet, now I trembled, as if I would die.

"The transfiguration and the resurrection appearances of my master had been of the *man* Jesus. But what I saw, now, in heaven was Jesus, as *God!*

"And yet," (John paused here and closed his eyes at the memory), "I knew Jesus still loved me! Even in all of his wondrous splendor, I felt it. He reached out and touched me, as a friend. He touched me on the shoulder." (John reached across and unconsciously fingered the spot where Jesus had touched him.) "And for all his majesty, that touch was familiar. It was the hand of my master, felt often as we had accompanied him on earth. It was a common gesture we had enjoyed of the man we had looked up to and served, for so long.

"I also heard my mentor's voice—not the peal of thunder that had first greeted me at the beginning of the vision. It was now my friend's voice that said, 'Do not be afraid.' I can't explain it, but in that moment, I knew Jesus was saying to me, 'You have nothing to fear, here. You belong here. This is who I AM, and you are still mine. So now, let's get to work. You need to take in all of this, so you can write it down.'"

John sat tall in his chair, now, his expression serious.

"And the two of you," John said pointing a finger at Anna and me, "are part of the reason I was to write the vision. I know you have read my writings. But you need to read them, again. And think of me as I saw it all, that first time."

We nodded.

"I'm old, now," John continued. "And even you are old, my young friends. It is your children and grandchildren who need to know the stories of Jesus and my vision. You need to impress on them that everything I and others have written is true. Tell them while there is still time that Jesus is not far away. He never has been. And he is coming again, soon!"

John finally gave up storytelling for the night, and Anna and I tucked him into the first comfortable bed he had slept in for many painful years. We watched him sleep for a few minutes before we retired.

What a privilege Anna and I have had to know John and to see Jesus and hear him, firsthand. I thrill to think that one day we will see the fulfillment of John's glorious visions. The thread of earthly history will draw to a close, only to open on the fabric of a new frontier with Jesus, our friend and our God. I can hardly wait!

3

SET FREE

I first saw Rick when I started work at PC Industries. I flirted, of course. As receptionist I saw everyone who came through the front doors, and Rick wasn't the first to flirt back. I purred when I hooked him. Rick knew I was married (I never bothered to remove my wedding ring), but he didn't seem to care. And I wasn't above a little fun. It was perfectly harmless, of course.

My friend, Susannah, didn't like it. She warned me not to get involved. "You shouldn't play around," she said. "Especially with this guy; Rick is running for state senator. In addition to wrecking your marriage, you could wreck his political career."

I just laughed. Rick and I were always discreet. I covered my tracks well. No one, especially my husband, would ever know.

I enjoyed the heady power of seduction. I knew I was attractive; I had always turned heads, even in high school. That's when Ed and I had first met. Actually, we had met in our worship youth group, and we had both sung on a special music team. Ed had followed me around like a puppy. And I had loved that I could twist him around my little finger. Everybody assumed we would get married, and we did.

Marriage to Ed was okay. But what little spark I had felt in the beginning had faded quickly. The excitement of the conquest was gone. But Ed was security, and I wasn't about to let that go.

I soon learned, however, that I still had the power. A man behind me in line at the Sub World diner came on to me with a tentative comment. And a guy in the grocery store asked if I knew where to find the pizza sauce, and then he stood talking for several minutes. I was flattered, and such attentions stirred me up inside.

At first, I stayed true to Ed. After all, I did care about him. And I had made a commitment to him. And I did believe extra-marital affairs were wrong. We had both grown up on what was right and wrong. It had been part of my worship school background, and I believed fidelity should matter.

But one day, a man from the worship group started paying attention to me. While I waited in the assembly room for Ed to finish talking with friends back in the lesson room, Don made his way over to chat. I soon realized he sought me out every chance he got. We would discuss his recent divorce, and I would sympathize with him. And next thing I knew, he and I were meeting for coffee on the nights when Ed was at worship administration meetings. Our meet ups led to the inevitable, and I thrived on the excitement of the secrecy and the attention.

Ed never found out. And as far as I knew, no one from the worship group knew about it, either. And eventually, the affair faded away.

But the ease of it had numbed my sense of values. I found myself responding to various other come-ons in hopes of another fling, which, of course, happened.

Then when I started working, there were more opportunities than ever. I assumed Rick would simply be the first.

Rick and I usually met at a remote motel in a nearby town. We registered under assumed names and paid cash. Our excuse to the night clerk who saw us often and thought we were married, was that we'd been to a concert or theater production in the city and liked to make a full night of it away from our (imaginary) kids. He would joke with us about how lucky we were to get away, since he was stuck working nights.

It was easy to fool Ed. He trusted me, and I told him my company was sending me to various training events so I could learn more about the computers we made. Ed always accepted my excuses, without question. No one but my friend Susannah had any inkling of my activities. Susannah tried to be my conscience. "How can you sit in worship hour with Ed and act like nothing is happening?" she would ask. And I would glibly spout something like, "Can I help it if God made me with the looks and the need for attention?"

And I never gave God another thought. He was just a storybook character I had heard about in worship group since childhood. I didn't necessarily doubt God's existence, but I didn't truly think he was interested in my fun.

One day, Ed made plans for us to go hear a new religious speaker. I had seen reports about the man on the news. This *John* person was an oddball who ranted about repentance and coming back to God. I was surprised Ed wanted to hear him. Besides, the guy refused to come into town to hold his meetings. You had to drive out to find him, then finish on foot on a rough, unpaved trail. And once you got there, you had to sit or stand in the hot sun. I wasn't looking forward to it.

When we set out, I marveled at the number of people crowding down that uneven, winding path to the river. I overheard snatches of conversation, along the way.

One older woman was telling her friend, "I've waited all my life for someone to call God's people to account. Our society, today, has become entirely too lax in our lifestyles and our worship. John says God is giving us a chance to make it right with him, just like he did in the days of the prophets. And it's up to us to respond and repent and turn back to him."

The younger woman asked if the older woman was planning to have John baptize her. The younger woman added, "I hear John urges baptism and hundreds of people have already done it to show their repentance."

The older woman exclaimed, "Yes, I'll be baptized! I know I need washing from my sins, like everybody else."

I wondered: *Was Ed planning to be baptized?* He had said nothing about it, but I suspected this had been his plan all along.

Well, I thought, *Ed can follow the crowd if he wants to, as long as he doesn't expect me to get my hair wet over some eccentric preacher. It's bad enough I've already turned my ankle on this stupid path. Why can't this guy hold a meeting in an amphitheater or a football field that doesn't require a sweaty nature hike?*

At the river's edge, I got my first look at this *John* character. And was he a sight! He evidently didn't believe in anything modern. He looked like a caveman, dressed in animal skins and with wild hair and a beard I doubted had ever been cut or combed.

He probably lives in a cave, I decided. *Figures! Religious fanatics are always weird.*

I marveled, again, at the number of people who waded down to him. I could hear their long confessions of sin before the zealot dragged them through the water. Person after person then re-climbed the bank with a look of peace on their faces. For some reason, I was jealous of that peace. But it was foolishness, of course. Religion was just wishful thinking.

I felt Ed reach for my hand to draw me forward in the line with him toward the baptizer, and I curled my fingers so they slipped away. I met his surprised eye with a slight shake of my head and what I hoped came across as a shy smile. Ed looked wistful, but he left me and moved forward, alone.

I watched, impatiently, in the sun's heat as Ed and others inched ahead. The closer people got to the river the less they talked.

Then, I observed an incident involving a man John hesitated to take into the water. I strained to hear their exchange, and I gathered that the prophet felt this man didn't need baptizing. *How odd!* I chuckled. *Somebody with nothing to repent of?*

In the end, John did baptize the man—a man who came out of the water with a flash of light and a rumble from the sky. People standing nearest the river gazed about them, in surprise.

Then, curiously, the stranger exited by way of the far bank

and started into the desert. He walked until he disappeared, and I wondered: *Where is that guy going? There's nothing for miles in that direction. Evidently, he's as touched in the head as the prophet.*

I shook my head. *Hurry up, Ed! This is all silliness.*

A wet and energized Ed caught up with me after his dunking. Breathlessly, he asked, "Did you see the man John baptized—the man who walked up the other side of the river bank? Someone said his name is *Jesus.* They didn't know much about him, but he certainly captured our attention with that dove fluttering over his head and the voice from heaven addressing the baptizer."

Although curious to know more, I smiled indulgently and nodded. I didn't want to encourage Ed. He was already too deep into this religious stuff.

I wanted to go home.

A storm of religious hysteria hung over the towns around us, now. Strangers, and people we knew, spread word about the healer named Jesus. They said Jesus not only healed but claimed to be the son of God. I watched people I had known all my life buy a tankful of gas and leave their jobs to travel after Jesus and listen to him preach. It had to be mass hypnotism!

News reporters mocked the flocking crowds. And orthodox religious leaders snickered and called the people "gullible fools."

First John, the baptizer, and now Jesus, I thought. *What was the world coming to?*

And then, one day, Ed appeared on the TV screen defending the growing movement.

Ed tried to convince the reporter that Jesus was everything the crowds said he was. Leaning into the microphone, Ed asked, "Have you listened to Jesus, yourself? He's offering sound advice for living—not the mumbo-jumbo we usually get. And he's doing something for the people who are hurting. He's making a difference!"

Ed was so weak! And I was so embarrassed!

To wash the disgust out of my system, I called Rick and suggested we meet at the usual place. I knew Rick could be counted on to be normal.

After our night together, I hated to leave, but I knew I couldn't stay with Rick. I needed to go to work, and Rick needed to get out and win his campaign. Unfortunately for Rick, the media focused little attention on him. Jesus was drawing the publicity, these days. Or, so I thought.

I learned differently, the minute I opened the motel room door. A press of news people with cameras and microphones surged forward, and I retreated in panic and slammed the door.

"Rick!" I cried. "We're in trouble!"

Rick peeked under a corner of the curtain and moaned, "Oh, no!" Then, under his breath, he muttered, "I'm ruined!"

Those outside banged on the door. "Come on out! We know you're in there, Mr. Cleary," they hollered.

Rick rolled his eyes at the ceiling and groaned. He fell back, onto the bed.

But he sighed and sat up, again. I guess he figured he might as well face the music; this wasn't going away. Rick ordered me to stay inside, and he opened the door to go out.

It proved a mistake. The reporters and a camera operator threw the door wide and barged past Rick to where I stood in the back of the room.

"Well, what have we here?" one rude reporter chortled. "Look who the good Mr. Cleary has been seeing! If it isn't the wife of that Jesus-lover, Ed Stump!"

The reporter taunted me with the microphone, and the camera hung within inches of my face.

Rick shoved the reporter aside and grabbed my arm. "Come on!" he commanded, and I stumbled after him out of the room. Rick pushed me into the car and then waded back through the mass of media to collect our suitcases. With great difficulty, he got them into the trunk and climbed into the car. The reporters scattered when they realized Rick wasn't going to stop for anyone in his way. And in a couple of minutes, we were racing down the highway toward home.

Neither of us said a word.

When we got to the mall at the edge of town, Rick drove to where I had parked my car. For some reason, there were people everywhere, and I wondered why. Who or what was at the mall, today, to draw this crowd?

Fortunately, their attention was elsewhere. Rick pulled out my suitcase and put it into my trunk, and I stood fumbling for my car keys. Rick said, "I'm sorry, Sharon. We've both made a mess of things. I hope Ed can forgive us." With that, he turned to go to his car. But the focus of the crowd had changed, and Rick couldn't budge.

News reporters, who had been hanging around the edge of the mall event, now set upon Rick with their microphones. They had somehow put together who we were and why we were here. I imagined a hundred cell phone texts flying between the reporters we had left at the hotel and those here. The mall media circled us like a pack of wild dogs.

The townspeople turned, too, to see who the reporters had spotted. Someone shouted, "Hey! It's Cleary and Mrs. Stump. Looks like they've been spending some time together. Whooeee! Wait until Ed hears this!"

And then, the worst happened. The crowd parted and pushed Ed through to where we stood.

Why was Ed here? I wondered.

And one of the crowd's hecklers called out, "Hey, Mr. Reporter! Here's the husband, now. Does he know about his wife's hanky-panky with Cleary?"

Ed's stricken face tore at my heart. *What have I done?* I groaned.

The reporter hounding Rick recognized Ed. "Say," he said, turning the camera around and sticking it in Ed's face, "I recognize you! You're the guy who sticks up for this so-called religious miracle-worker, Jesus! You're in luck! Seems we've been able to help you catch your wife playing under-the-covers with the senator-to-be. Since you're so holy, what have you got to say about it?"

A strangled sob escaped from Ed, and he fell back.

As he did, however, unidentified arms appeared under Ed's arms and supported him from behind, and the arms moved with Ed into the forefront of the media melee. Then I saw the owner of the arms: it was Jesus!

My first thought was, *Well, that explains the crowd and why Ed is here.* But then I wondered why Jesus had left his platform to come to the parking lot.

Had he come to confront us, too? Or had Jesus meant to interrupt the media frenzy around Ed and draw the attention to himself? In either case, Jesus had succeeded.

The rabid reporter who had attacked Ed, now pounced on Jesus: "Well, Mr. Religious, himself! What do you think we ought to do, here, with these awful sinners? Should we tar and feather them? Or string them up? Or...?"

The healer stood, calm. I marveled that Jesus didn't rise to the bait or take advantage of the publicity opportunity. Nor did he confront Rick and me.

Instead, Jesus asked to borrow Ed's cell phone. Ed fumbled in his pocket and passed the phone to him. For the next couple of minutes, Jesus focused his attention on the phone's tiny screen. His thumbs punched in a message and several contact numbers. And then, he hit *Send.*

I know it was *Send* because all over the crowd and throughout the media, cell phones began to ring and vibrate, and people grabbed at their pockets to answer them.

Eyes that fixed on the little screens grew wide with surprise.

What had Jesus written? I wondered. *And how had he known all those cell numbers?*

Three phones had not rung: those of the camera operator and two of the reporters. The three men continued to pepper Jesus with their questions and suggestions of what to do with "the adulteress and the adulterer."

Undisturbed, Jesus looked up from Ed's phone and leaned into one of the microphones. He said, "If any of you is without sin, let that person be the first to accuse these two and destroy them."

The reporters looked at one another. *What was that supposed to mean?*

Then, their cell phones began to ring. I watched them tap their screens, and as they read, their mouths opened in surprise. The camera lens dropped to face the ground, and the preoccupied reporters forgot their mission.

No one in the crowd or among the media looked up, any longer. All hung their heads in silence. They wanted nothing more to do with Jesus or with us. One by one, the multitude turned and slunk away.

As the parking lot emptied, Jesus looked up, and I found myself held captive in his gaze.

No wonder people regarded Jesus as extraordinary, I thought. *Those eyes see more about me than I have ever revealed to anyone or even acknowledged to myself.*

And yet, I was not afraid for him to know me. While I felt hot shame, and justly so, I did not feel cold judgment.

Jesus took Ed's arm and asked, "Sharon, who of this crowd condemns you?"

I looked at where the crowd had stood. Through a pool of tears, I replied, "No one, sir." (I called him "sir," because I didn't know what else to call him to show my respect.)

But wait! There was one who could rightfully condemn me.

Before I could stammer the amendment to my statement from "No one, sir" to "My husband, sir," Jesus declared, "Then neither do I condemn you."

A judge commuting a sentence: that's the closest thing I can relate to his words. I felt I had done *him* wrong and deserved to be held accountable to *him*. And accordingly, *he* was forgiving me.

And then, with a wave of his arm that took in Rick and me, Jesus said, "Go, now, and leave your life of sin."

Rick deflated and dropped to Jesus's feet. And I stood quaking.

I forced my eyes to look up, to see Ed's face. That's where I would find my judgment. I had sinned and broken his heart.

But Ed met my gaze with tears of love!

In disbelief, I fell to the ground and kissed my husband's feet. Instead of lording it over me, as he had every right to do, Ed was forgiving me!

Together, in cleansing tears, we worshipped at Jesus's feet.

Then, Jesus placed his hands on our heads. Unlike others who had followed Jesus, I had never watched him heal with his touch. But I know now how that touch feels.

Jesus's touch opened my eyes to recognize the deceit of my heart for what it had always been: dark and ugly and twisted, with fingers that had metastasized through my spirit. I repented with all my being. And with Jesus's hand still upon me, my tumor of seduction and lust shrank away, and, with it, my shame. My darkness receded, and light filled every crevice of my soul.

I never saw Rick, again. My guess is that he got into his car and kept driving.

Ed and I fell in love—for real, this time—with a common foundation in Jesus.

And I remain caught up in the Jesus I met that day.

How different Jesus was from my former conception of God. My former God, at worst, had been a fearful and awful judge and, at best, an indifferent or imaginary being—a boogeyman invented by parents and religious leaders to keep me in line.

Now, however, I see God as the holy and loving father of Jesus. I see God as righteous and filled with anger at sin but also filled with pity and love for deluded and broken souls. And I see a God so bent on restoring and reclaiming sinners that he sent his son, Jesus, to overcome sin on our behalf.

Ed and I mourned when Jesus suffered our penalty to remove our sin and shame. And then we rejoiced when Jesus took up his life again to prove he had won the victory.

My husband and I work side-by-side, now, to teach others about Jesus and his grace. We share joyfully that what is lost can be found, what is broken can be healed, what is captive can be set free, and what is dead can be reborn to live forever.

I speak from experience. I have known Jesus's touch. In my testimony, I tell others how I stood, one day, condemned for adultery in a parking lot, but Jesus saved me. He set me free!

4

DREAMS

Did you know blind people can dream?

Many people think we don't because they associate dreams with visual images. But I have had dreams— lots of dreams—even though born blind.

In my dreams, I *see* the faces of my family and friends by the feel of their noses and cheeks and chins. I hear their voices and smell their colognes. And I dream of moving safely through my neighborhood with Goliath.

In my favorite dreams, I'm eating. I've been to the bakery on my way to the bus stop, and I'm savoring a honey bun or a cruller and washing it down with a cup of coffee.

Sometimes, I gain super powers in my dreams and overcome great obstacles. But I've had nightmares, too. In those, I'm falling toward an unknown bottom. I'm not only blind but I've grown deaf, and I feel the claws and teeth of whatever is about to eat me. Thankfully, just in time, Goliath's growls rumble through my bones, and he pulls me back to safety.

And, one night, I dreamed a very different dream. That night, I *saw* heaven and light. I *saw* God.

In that dream, I heard God say his son was visiting earth and had become the Son of David. God's words excited me. From childhood, I had learned that when the Son of David came, he would make every wrong right again. He would cure sickness and hurts and blindness with his touch. In my dream I heard the Son of David on the earth and heard crowds of people following him wherever he went.

When I awakened, I wanted to dream that dream again. But of course, it would not come. I have kept the memory of it alive, however, by thinking on it often, as I do this morning while getting dressed.

Goliath nudges me. His inner clock is infallible. He knows it is time to leave for the bus stop to go to the mall.

At the mall, I will spend my day listening. Most people will pass me by without a word, but some shoppers will stop for a moment. They will ask how I am and tell me about their families. At noon I will buy lunch, and then I will resume listening. After supper at the mall, I will ride the bus home. My routine seldom changes.

This morning, I select a chocolate-frosted donut from the bakery and carry it with my coffee to the bus stop. It's a balmy spring day, and I enjoy the sun's warmth on my face. But I also sense Goliath's unease. My protector is on alert.

I hear nothing out of place until a moment later. Then I hear what Goliath has already heard: a crowd coming down the sidewalk.

As I listen, I pinch myself. *Yes, I'm still awake.*

I pinch myself again because, although I am still blind, I *see* heaven and light. And I *see* God. And I *see* his son, the Son of David. And I *hear* the crowds of people who follow him.

And I recognize the crowd.

The crowd on the sidewalk, this morning, is the same crowd I heard in my special dream. I am sure of it.

I stand quickly and spill my coffee. Goliath edges closer, sensing something unusual is happening.

The crowd draws near, and I feel sure the Son of David is there, somewhere, just as in my dream.

People pass closely, now, and their clothing brushes me. I grab a handful of someone's jacket and stop them to ask, "Who are you following?" And they tell me, "Jesus is here. We're following him to where he is going to teach, next."

I release my hold on the jacket, and I cry out in my loudest voice, "Jesus! Son of David! Give me your mercy!"

The person I had grabbed shushes me. "He's not the Son of David," he says.

But I won't be shushed. I bellow in my best bass voice, "Jesus! Son of David! Please stop!" I am energized. I keep shouting, and the people around me hiss their annoyance.

But then, the crowd grows still. I sense someone nearing.

Goliath's tail beats against my legs.

"I am Jesus," a voice says, and my heart leaps. *It is the voice from my dream!*

"What is it you want me to do for you?" the Son of David says.

And I blurt out, "Lord, I want to see!"

"Ah!" says the man, and he rests a reassuring hand on my arm. Another hand covers my forehead. "So, receive your sight," he declares. "Your faith has healed you."

Instantly, my dream turns real!

My breath catches as the darkness disappears. Light floods in. And colors and movement dizzy me.

My eyes follow the hand I still feel on my forehead to a face. His face. The face of the Son of David. Out of habit, I reach out my fingers to touch that face.

And now I can see what my fingers feel.

You might not think fingers can capture expressions and feelings, but they can. And my newly opened eyes confirm a kindness I had already traced.

I can't look away. There is nothing I want to see in this moment but the face of the Son of David. And I cry, "Thank you!" as I bow before him.

Goliath licks my cheek, and I turn to see my big, shaggy dog. For the first time, I see his hairy face and pink tongue. And I see what I have often felt against my legs: his great wagging tail.

I laugh. And Jesus laughs. "He's quite an animal," he says.

Jesus roughs Goliath's ears and scratches his chin. And I get up and look around at the people, the shops, and the bench where I have waited for the bus. My world has changed. My dark fence is gone. I am free to go anywhere and free to do anything!

But there's nowhere I want to go and nowhere I want to be, except with Jesus. I want to follow the Son of David throughout the earth to watch him heal and put things right.

Jesus smiles and accepts my company.

So, as the crowd moves on, Jesus, Goliath, and I lead the way. And people smile as we pass.

I see my bus come and go. I see the sky and the clouds and the sun. And I see more people join the band of Jesus's followers that ends up at the city park. There, Jesus stops to teach.

I watch his face as his words paint a world where souls can be reborn; and then his healing touch demonstrates it. I peer into the eyes of those who listen and catch his dream. And I rejoice that one day the entire world will awaken to see heaven and light, and see God, and be healed by the Son of David.

5

STANDING TALL

One hour before the graduation ceremony would begin in the gymnasium, six-foot-seven tall "Tiny" snatched my cap and flung it into the basketball hoop. It snagged the netting and hung there. Only a sinker could get it out.

"Oh, tough one!" the others on the team tsk'd in mock sympathy. "But you can get it out if you make a good shot."

They tossed me a ball and then traipsed out of the gym giggling. Every so often I knew they peeked in the doorway to check on my progress because I heard gales of laughter from the hallway.

I tried, but I never got the ball anywhere near high enough to touch the hoop, let alone go into it. That's what happens when you're not even four feet tall and your arms are dwarfed like the rest of you.

I was humiliated when guests started to arrive and Coach Ferrell had to shoot my cap out of the hoop. Several people expressed amusement at what they saw as a harmless joke. But I wasn't laughing. This was only the latest of the bullying I'd endured all my life. And I was planning my revenge.

My dad, who died when I was young, had always been ashamed of me. There had never been a dwarf in the family before, and he was angry that he had produced a son "who could not be respected and amount to anything." My mother had coddled me before she had died, which hadn't helped. I now lived alone and stayed to myself.

In three years, I would inherit my uncle's house and a sizable bequest. My uncle had always liked me, perhaps because he wasn't very tall, either. But he had been smart and had made good money on the stock exchange. I shared his ability with numbers.

Three years. I prayed the time would fly.

In the meantime, I learned everything I could about the tribute-tax system. I had decided to become a tax collector.

Everyone had to pay the tax. Everyone, including Tiny and the rest of the ball team. It was a hated assessment because it went to the country that had absorbed ours after the war. Although the foreign sovereigns let our local religious authorities rule everyday life, everyone had to pay a hefty annual tax.

Those who collected taxes were locals who worked without a government paycheck. Collectors were allowed to charge an over-and-above amount for themselves from each assessment. As long as the sovereigns got their money, they didn't care what the tax collectors gleaned. And everyone knew tax collectors lived well.

With my uncle's inheritance, I would live well above the means of anyone else in town. I wouldn't need the income from tax collecting. But I didn't want the money; I wanted the position. As a tax collector I could command recognition and respect. And I got it.

I gloated at the surprise in neighbors' eyes the first time they discovered me sitting in the collection booth at the headquarters. And I smelled the fear in townspeople who replayed their ill-treatment of me in the past. They recognized the power I now wielded, and they dreaded the threat I posed.

Everyone scraped and bowed and called me "Sir." They inquired about my health and asked how my day was going. I would offer a supercilious smile and say, "How kind. I'm doing well, thank you." And then I would gouge them on their taxes. And they were helpless to say anything about it because of the guards at the door.

I made sure I charged certain people more than others—people like Tiny, Wesley, and Morgan. Everyone paid extra, but these three paid more.

I did have a heart, however. Mrs. Perch and old-man Garvey experienced my mercy. Those two lived on a pittance, and their tax assessments would have left them on the streets to starve. I made them pay me only one penny each, and I collected the rest from Tiny, Wesley, and Morgan. The only stipulation I made Mrs. Perch and Mr. Garvey agree to was to tell no one. After all, I had a reputation to uphold.

At first, I enjoyed my power. When I rode down the street in my limousine, people nodded in feigned politeness. And I acknowledged my subjects by nodding back. My vengeance was everything I had hoped for—except that for five years I worked and lived without one friend.

Although I lacked for nothing, my life, like my uncle's mansion, was empty. No one visited or accepted invitations to my parties. I attempted to befriend the religious authorities, but they wanted nothing to do with me. They spat that I worked for the sovereigns as a *money-grubbing traitor,* while they righteously rose to accept the burden of *buffer between* the sovereigns and the people. These self-righteous *buffers* labeled me a sinner of the first rank.

You might think other tax collectors would be my friends, but it was not so. No collector would mingle with me after my advancement to Chief Tax Collector. Although I had not sought the title, the appointment set me apart from my colleagues and made me suspect.

So, while top chefs from around the country fed me, and an army of valets and butlers and chauffeurs clothed, served, and drove me, I had no one to talk to or socialize with. I was more isolated and alone, now, than I had been before I took the job.

I knew my revenge was killing me, but I saw no way to turn things around. Nothing could undo the dynamic of my former life, and I saw no way out of the mess I had made of my present life. Day after day, I collected money and went home to nothing. After dinner, I retired to my den and watched the news and a movie. And then I went to bed. I wore my loneliness like a shroud.

Then, one day, as I ate my gourmet breakfast and my butler tuned in the morning news, I sat up in surprise. A reporter was interviewing a man accompanied by a large, wiry-haired dog that I recognized as Goliath.

Goliath belonged to Bart, the blind man from the mall. In a weak moment, yesterday, I had stopped to talk to him. And I feel guilty about it because I took advantage of him—but not in the way you might be thinking. I took advantage of his blindness to have someone to talk to.

As a blind man, Bart could not see my trappings as a tax collector. Nor could he see my dwarfed stature. To him, I was just another person passing by and saying hello. I had asked him something about his dog, and soon we were chatting like old friends.

It was refreshing to talk with someone who hadn't pre-judged me before I'd sat down. I even remember laughing with him about something. I had not laughed with anyone in years, and it brought tears to my eyes.

But it couldn't last. A woman passing by whispered loudly (on purpose?) to her companion, "Look at that! The dwarf tax collector talking to a blind man!"

I knew Bart had heard her because I saw his brow briefly form a question. But he said nothing, and I rose to leave. That's when Bart asked if he could touch my face.

I hesitated.

"I want to remember you," he said. "My fingers will paint your picture for me."

What could it hurt? I sat across from him and let his fingers brush my features.

He smiled.

"Thank you, friend," he said. "You have a kind face. Can you tell me your name?"

Again, I hesitated. If Goliath had not put his chin on my knee for a pat on the head, I wouldn't have answered. But I said, "Zak. My name is Zak. And I need to be going."

Bart gripped my hand. "Zak," he said, "I am glad you stopped.

Goliath and I appreciate friends who take time to chat with us. I hope we will see you again."

See me again, he said. I knew it was just a figure of speech, but it shamed me to be glad he could not see me. We would never be *friends* in the normal way because of who he was and because of who I am.

I bid him goodbye and left him with the impression we would meet and talk again. But I knew we never would.

The camera on the television news zeroed in on Bart's face, and I listened as Bart answered the reporter's questions.

"And when Jesus passed by," Bart was saying, "I called out to him, and he stopped."

The reporter interrupted. "Do you mean to say that Jesus, surrounded by so many people, heard you and stopped in response to your call?"

Bart laughed. "I have to admit that I didn't just 'call' in a normal voice. I bellowed with every bit of lung-power I could generate. I wanted to be heard above the crowd."

"So," said the reporter, "he stopped. And then what?"

Bart's face lit up. "He healed me! That's what!"

"I don't understand," the reporter said. "What do you mean, he healed you?"

Bart replied, "I asked Jesus to heal my blindness, and he did."

The reporter didn't believe Bart had been blind earlier this morning. "Blind?" he said. "How long had you been blind? Was it temporary, from an accident?"

"No accident," said Bart. "I was born blind, and doctors had given me no hope. Goliath has been my eyes for a long time."

The dog looked up at the mention of its name.

"So," said the reporter, "you are no longer blind. What will you do, now, since you can no longer draw disability (at least I assume you've told the authorities to discontinue your disability)?"

Bart smiled. "Of course, I'll report it. And I'll draw out my savings and use the money to go wherever my friend Jesus goes."

"Ah!" said the reporter. "Interesting."

The reporter turned away from Bart and faced the camera. He said, "Jesus, the healer, arrived on the outskirts of the city a short while ago, and, already, people are claiming he's healed them. His bus is making its way over to Main Street where thousands of people have gathered to see him. It is unknown whether he will remain in town or just pass through. We'll bring you coverage as events unfold." The field reporter signed off and the desk reporter picked up to introduce another topic.

I jerked the napkin from my neck and ordered my butler to turn off the program and call for my valet.

"Hurry! Help me dress," I ordered when I got to my room.

Before the valet could remove my bathrobe, I shouted for the butler to call my driver. I wanted to get to Main Street. I wanted to see this Jesus who had healed my friend from the mall. I wondered what Jesus looked like. And I wondered if I might see Bart, again.

In minutes, my car came as close as we could get to the lower end of Main Street. Thousands of people jammed the area and made it impossible to pass. I ordered my driver through some alleys to look for space at the other end of the street.

But no matter how far up we went, people crowded the curbs and sidewalks. I could see nothing from the car, and I was too short to see over people if I mixed with the crowd. If only I were taller!

Then, I spied a tree with a low-hanging branch that spread over the heads of the people at the curb. The branch seemed just thick enough to hold someone my size, so I ordered my driver to get out of the car and lift me up.

Boris never hesitated; he always did whatever I asked. After all, I paid him handsomely for his services. Without questioning, Boris hoisted me onto his shoulders, and from there I scrambled onto the branch and scooted out over the heads of the people at the edge of the street. *Click! I steadied my cell phone on the branch and tested it with a sample picture.*

Some children, below, spotted me and pointed, and their parents snickered when they saw me in the tree in my good suit and tie. But I didn't care.

For nearly a half-hour I straddled the branch. And then my wait was rewarded. I saw the top of a bus and heard the distant crowds cheer. Soon, I would catch a glimpse of Jesus.

Despite the cheering tumult, I was safe in the tree. Parents drew their children into their arms or onto their shoulders to protect them from trampling as the bus drew near.

Click! I captured photos of the bus's approach. Then, the cheers of the crowd became deafening when the vehicle drew opposite my tree and stopped. A passenger in the front seat hung out the window and high-fived dozens of upheld hands. *Click! I took a picture.* Then, a posse of large men climbed out and formed a barrier around that passenger door. From my perch, I could see it all.

The man who left the bus moved to my side of the road, and I noted how ordinary he looked. But I knew greatness isn't measured by looks.

Was he Jesus? I hoped so. He was standing, now, at the foot of my tree. I celebrated that I had picked a good spot.

Jesus looked up, as if he had seen me above him. He raised his hand for quiet, and the crowd nearest him grew still. They were expecting him to speak, and no one wanted to miss a word.

Jesus looked up, again, and I smiled. It was perfect! *Click! I snapped the picture on my cell phone and waited to hear what Jesus would share with everyone.*

Instead, Jesus addressed me. My astonished ears heard, "Zak! Come down. You need to get things ready. I'm coming to your house."

In mid-click, I lost hold of the cell phone and watched as it tumbled through the air. Just before it hit the pavement, Jesus rescued it.

I nearly fell, too! Jesus knew my name!

I heard whispers hiss through the knots of people below me: "Jesus doesn't know what kind of man that dwarf is!"

Some people tried to shout and tell him I was a tax collector.

But Jesus ignored them all and waited while Boris settled me onto the ground.

Click! Jesus clicked a selfie with me! Then he slipped the phone into my pocket and said, "We'll meet you there."

The astonished crowd made a hole for Jesus to re-enter the bus and for Boris and me to get to our car. As we drove away, I marveled when Boris actually said something. (The man seldom spoke a word.)

Boris observed, "That man must be special."

That's an understatement, I thought. But out loud I said, "Yes. And he's coming to my house!" Then I added quietly, "And I don't deserve it!"

In the rearview mirror, I saw eyebrows raise. But my chauffeur said nothing more.

We arrived at the house, and I shouted for my staff. From the stair landing, I ordered them to prepare for an unknown number of people who were to arrive any moment and would need food and places to sit. "Pretend it's a party," I said.

Stunned, the staff stood for a moment, until I ordered them, "Get moving! They'll be here at any minute!"

My butler, the best in the business, clicked his heels, straightened his collar, and boomed out orders that sent everyone scattering. Chairs appeared from storage for placement on the lawn and around the ballroom table. Gardeners were dispatched to bring armloads of flowers to fill the massive vases in the entry. Vegetable gardeners raced to collect fruit and vegetables from the trees and vines next to the kitchen. Chefs pulled meat from the smokehouse, and bakers began kneading quick doughs and rolling out pies. China and silverware clattered onto the table to be properly placed by the dining stewards, and the chief steward ran to select the appropriate wines from the cellar. Activity filled every square inch of the downstairs. And Boris must have shared the name of our guest because I heard whispers: "It's the healer! Jesus is coming to the house."

I retreated to my bedroom suite, upstairs, and stood in the relative quiet of my balcony overlooking my woods and up into the sky. Was this really happening?

A short time later, I raced across the hall to look out the front window. There, I watched as scores of people relinquished their car keys to my servants and walked into my house.

For years, I had longed to entertain with parties and lunches on the lawn. But everyone had despised me. I had given them every reason to hate me. And now they were coming—because Jesus was coming!

I hurried downstairs to receive my honored guest. With perfect manners, Jesus nodded to me, and I took his hand and led him into my ballroom. In spite of such short notice, the room looked perfect! I seated Jesus at the head of the table, and I had my staff bring my special raised chair to the foot. I had never used this table, and I regretted to see Jesus miles away from me on the other end.

I let the butler decide how to arrange the guests—except for Bart. I had whispered that I wanted Bart next to me, with his dog at his feet.

The stewards poured the wine, and all guests turned to await my toast. I raised my glass, but instead of a toast, I offered a prayer: "God, thank you for my guests and thank you for your bounty. We celebrate you this day. Amen!" Everyone lifted their glasses toward heaven and sipped their wine.

Once the soup came, those around the table engaged in conversation. It was time for me to acknowledge those seated beside me. I turned first to my right. Before I spoke, Bart said, "Hello, Zak. It's good to see you again."

This time, his comment about *seeing me* was no mere figure of speech. Bart could see me, for real.

"I'm thankful you can see me," I said.

Then I stuttered my admission. "I didn't think we would see each other after our visit, yesterday. I apologize. I planned to avoid you, because I couldn't bear to have you come to resent me, like everyone else does."

But Bart said, "You should not have worried. The man I met

yesterday was a kind man. Sad, I thought, but kind. Sometimes those who have lost their sight see things others do not. What I saw was a man who needed a friend and who was looking for a certain something that had eluded him."

How true, I thought. I had been looking for a friend, and I had been searching for an indescribable something for a long time.

Bart's next words surprised me.

"Jesus is that something," he said. "I knew it the moment he healed me. I knew he was more than just a healer. He is a man from God, like no other. And his mission is to change people—to change them into what God has always intended them to be. Jesus gives people mercy and a second chance."

As Bart spoke, I glanced at the other end of the table to find Jesus looking at me. Although we were a mile apart in a room full of guests, I felt as if he saw only me. And I felt he was affirming what Bart had just said. I could almost hear Jesus saying, "I'm here to give you a second chance, Zak. Will you take it?"

The impression was so strong that a surge of adrenaline shot through me. My miserable life flashed before me like a bolt of lightning. And a thunder of resolve rose within me.

I did something I'd never done before: I scrambled to my feet and stood on the seat of my raised chair. Everyone turned to look at the dwarf on the chair. But I didn't care if they thought I was a dwarf. I cared what Jesus thought of me. In front of everyone I called out, "Jesus, I know you give second chances. And I want one, today. I, here and now, vow to give half of my possessions to the poor, and if I have cheated anybody out of anything, I will pay back four times the amount."

Murmurs filled the room. No one had ever heard of such a thing! A generous tax man!

I bowed my head to realize how many people I had hurt, and I wished I could crawl away and disappear.

But then, I heard Jesus's voice from the other end of the table say, "Take note, everyone. Today, God's salvation has come to this house.

This man, a child of God, was lost but has found his way. I am glad. This is my mission as the Son of Man—to seek out all who are lost and save them."

Jesus's words melted over me in blessing. And I felt something new from Jesus and from among my guests: I felt forgiven.

A man to my left, who had not yet spoken a word, said, "Well done, my friend. Your restitution restores my faith in God and his people."

And Bart beamed at me. His once sightless eyes glistened. "Indeed, my friend!" he said. "Indeed!"

I signaled for my butler. When he approached, I told him to order my accountant to make up the proper amounts and send them by messenger, immediately, to Tiny, Wesley, and Morgan. Other gifts, for other people, would follow, tomorrow. But, for now, I wanted these accounts clear. And I immediately felt the weight of my vengeance leave me. I felt taller than I had ever felt because I knew, in that moment, that the measure of a man is not in his height but in the condition of his heart.

6

MOTHER-IN-LAW

Yes, I admit I'm a typical mother-in-law. I tried to warn my daughter not to marry that man, but, of course, she did. With her father already gone, I had no way to stop her. Oh, well! That's how things are, sometimes.

But, you know? Peter didn't turn out too badly. I laugh when I think of his big, lumbering ways and his stomping through my little house in his oversized boots whenever he came courting. Oh, he was polite enough. And he took care not to chip my fine bone china tea set when I let the two of them have my dining room to themselves of an afternoon.

But even though he was no fine gentleman, he was good to my Alice. And Alice adored him. Even the dog liked him. So, what could I do? I smiled and liked him, too.

And once they married, I have to say I was glad. After all, his family had a bit of money. They owned fishing boats and part of a cannery. And he worked hard. You could tell he enjoyed being out on the water with his brother and other fishermen.

And he was good to me. Not all boys are good to their mothers-in-law, but this one was a good boy!

He tried to save my husband's house for me, but of course, he couldn't. I had no money or means to keep it. The religious leaders took it off my hands for a shamefully small price. I've always tried to be faithful to the leadership, but their dealings with widows is not always fair. I had thought the religious leaders were supposed to help widows and orphans, but instead, they often take advantage of us. They dole out only the smallest pittance in return for which we are supposed to be grateful. Hmmmf! While widows less fortunate than I live on soup and day-old bread, the leaders dine on prime rib and savory stuffing. And God doesn't seem to notice! (Not that I would say anything against God. He has a lot on His plate, you know?)

Well, in the end, Peter and Alice let me live in the back apartment of their house. Andrew, Peter's brother, lived in an upper apartment, and I, of course, lived in the mother-in-law's apartment. And I have loved it because it means my Alice is always near me.

Even so, such things don't always last. The marriage got a little shaky when Peter told Alice he and Andrew were joining a traveling ministry team and he would be away from home a lot. I didn't say, "I told you so," but that doesn't mean it wasn't on the tip of my tongue!

With all of his absences, however, Alice and I didn't really suffer. As I said, Peter wasn't poor. And we heard from him, every, single, day. In that way, he was a good boy.

Well, Alice went to see the ministry team in action a couple of times, and she came home with stories I found hard to believe. She claimed their leader, a man named Jesus, healed people. Ah, youth! They are so starry-eyed about life. She'll realize one of these days that things aren't always what they seem to be. But I said little, of course. I mean, who am I to burst the bubble of the naïve?

And then, one day, out of the blue, Peter sent word that he had invited Jesus to come to our house for dinner. I clasped my hands to my chest. Alice caught me before I passed out! Achhh! What did I know of entertaining such a person? I complained to our neighbor that we were going to entertain a very important person, and she commiserated with me.

"I know," Clarice said. "Nobody knows how much time and effort goes into such a thing. You poor dear! And you a widow! It is at least good your son-in-law has some fishing money. Otherwise, I don't know what you and Alice would do!"

She was right. I was fortunate, but, with such company coming, there was so much to do.

I girded up my skirts and sat at the kitchen table to write out a long grocery list. Of course, I wanted to pick up a good brisket from the butcher. And Alice swept out every corner of the house. We even bought a new door mat that said, "Bless those who pass here." (It's the latest thing in door mats, you know.)

And I cut up potatoes to mash and made an apple pie and a cake. And Alice made the green beans, creamed some corn, and cut up a huge salad. The yeast from my dinner rolls filled the air as the dough raised on the counter. I even pulled out some of my homemade strawberry jam and sweet pickles. Such a meal! I hoped that my meager offering would be excused.

Alice put the leaves in the dining room table and spread it with my best table cloth. I had last used that cloth when my husband was living and had his bosses over for supper. (Oh, poor Archie! I do miss him!)

Then, our sympathetic neighbor let us borrow her good dishes to add to mine. And I laid out everything as perfectly as I could. I guessed we were ready.

And then, it happened! It always happens that way, don't you know? I got the mother of all migraines! I was so ill I couldn't even see. And I had vertigo, and I was nauseated. Have you ever had such a thing? Why, oh why, did it have to happen, now? I couldn't serve our company! The most important company that had ever come to a person's house was coming to ours, and I was unable to even stand up!

And then, it got worse. I became fevered. I had never been fevered with a migraine, before. What was wrong with me? What an awful time to get sick!

Alice had been running back and forth to the microwave with my little migraine heating pillow, but now she exchanged it for an ice pack. Even so, I kept burning up. And I moaned when I heard the commotion of voices at the door. Peter's voice was loudest, of course. And why not? After all, he was here to show off his family to the important person he traveled with, and he had every right to expect his mother-in-law to be at the door, like a good hostess, with his wife. But, where was I? I was in my room dying.

Well, nobody had to know there was a mother-in-law, right? Peter had probably never mentioned me, anyway. After all, why should he? I was nothing—just a pile of needless burning flesh in a dark bedroom, waiting to die!

I heard Alice crying, and I heard Peter trying to understand what she was saying. Poor girl! She was worried about me—plus I'm sure she knew she couldn't manage such an important guest all by herself. She needed her husband's mother-in-law! It was foolishness to entertain anyone without the mother-in-law. Oh, if only I could stop sweating and keep the room from reeling about me, I could save the day. But I can only throw my hands in the air and ask, "Why, God? Why today?"

Because Peter had never learned how to whisper, I could hear him saying, "It's all right, Alice. We can manage without your mother, I'm sure."

And now I was *really* sick! Manage without me? I moaned in the realization that no one needed the mother-in-law.

But then, I heard another voice reply, rather loudly, "What! No mother-in-law? I don't think so! This poor woman who is your wife should not be expected to have to worry about her mother while she is taking care of us. We MUST have the mother-in-law."

And I almost felt better! Some young man, out there, had been raised to know the value of a mother-in-law. After I become well (if I ever do) I will make that man a cake.

It was then I heard the bedroom door fly open. And I heard that man call out, "What is all of this? Mothers-in-law do not get sick. Mothers-in-law are indispensable!"

He strode over to the bed and took my hand, and he cried out a prayer to God. "We need this woman well!" he announced to heaven. Then, he looked at me. "I say to you, mother-in-law, get up now, and tend to your business. You have company at your house!"

At his command, a wave overtook me like a flood, from the tips of my toes to the top of my head. My skin became cool, and my hair and clothes, which had been soaked with sweat, became dry and clean, as if I had just showered and dressed. I was recovered, and the man put out his hand to help me out of bed.

I was in his debt! A man who understood mothers-in-law and who had prayed me well.

He walked me from the bedroom down to the kitchen. There, Alice breathed a sigh of relief and pressed her hands together in gratefulness. The man and I nodded politely to one another, and he released me to my work.

I pulled the meat from the oven, surprised to find it not overdone, even though I had not been there to pull it out, earlier. And the potatoes were just right to be mashed. Alice brought out the beans and the salad. And with a flourish, I set everything on the table and announced to Peter that his guests could eat.

You should have seen Peter, Andrew, James, and John, when they saw the spread we had laid out and then heard me say, "If only I had known we were having such distinguished company, I would have made a special meal!"

I gave those boys the *mother-in-law stare* daring them to sputter one word to the contrary. They had eaten in this house often, and they knew this was not our usual fare. But they also knew, by my look, that they would never eat at this table, again, if they said anything about the fancy spread before them. I saw James swallow his tongue and duck behind Peter, and the other three looked to the floor with lips sealed. I nodded imperiously, and they all sat down.

Peter set my healer at the head of the table, and the healer prayed for the meal. I marveled that my healer was Jesus!

How he prayed! He spoke to God as if God was right here in our house. And I wondered at it. Never had I heard a man address God so familiarly and with such grace.

What a day it was! I couldn't wait to tell Clarice all about it. And when I did, our neighbor could hardly believe it!

Since then, Alice and I have told the story, repeatedly, of how my son-in-law knew the son of God as a mentor and friend, and how Jesus had come to our house and set things right by healing the mother-in-law so she could serve. And I sent my healer a cake, as I had said I would.

When tragic, and then wonderful events took place, later, it is no wonder that I understood why Peter felt he had to tell the world about this Jesus. And Alice traveled with him, with my blessing, of course. And Peter wrote me, often, from wherever they were—because, as I have always said, he is a good boy!

7

PAYMENT

"Of course, Jesus pays the required religious tax," I tossed over my shoulder. I gave the impression I wasn't at all worried about the impending deadline. (To myself I growled, *If I have to pay that tax, myself, it'll be paid! There is no way I'm waiting and possibly missing turning in that money before the big annual festival. Jesus has attracted enough negative press from the authorities. We're not going to stir up any more if I can help it!*)

I threw myself into the car and snorted to think a sniveling tax collector had hoped to put Jesus in a bad light by accosting me, in front of a crowd no less, and announcing Jesus hadn't yet paid his taxes. In the old days I would have cuffed the guy on the nose and sped away. But Jesus insists we "turn the other cheek." In my book, such things sound good in principle but aren't always satisfying in practice.

Oh, well. At least, I have Jesus's back. Heaven knows he needs somebody! He's always saying something to set the authorities on edge. I stick close in case one of those pompous dignitaries decides to try something drastic. They always talk "holier than thou," but when you get down to where some of those guys really live, you find them cheating a widow out of her last penny! Jesus needs to steer clear of them.

I was glad Jesus was relaxing at Andrew's and my house. Here, we could protect him. And my wife and mother-in-law were only too thrilled to entertain him. The other ten of Jesus's close companions were off relaxing with their families and friends, too, since we were in the area.

I stomped up the front steps, still debating whether to tell Jesus about my encounter with the tax man. It seemed better that I just take care of it and not bother Jesus. I would pay the taxes tomorrow and never mention it.

With this decided, Jesus caught me off guard when he brought up the subject. I hadn't even announced, "Hey, I'm back," before Jesus asked, "Peter, what do you think? From whom do earthly rulers take tax and tribute money? Their children or strangers?"

In surprise, I blurted out, "Not their kids!"

"So," Jesus said, "you're saying the children of the ruling household don't pay?"

I groaned. Was Jesus working around to saying he wasn't going to pay the tax? I was already picturing the uproar that would generate. He could even end up in jail!

I was *definitely* going to take care of this public relations nightmare. I would pay the tax, myself!

But Jesus wasn't finished. He said, "Even though we shouldn't have to pay, we can't set a bad example."

I breathed in relief. Maybe, Jesus was going to pay. Sometimes I had a hard time following him, especially when he talked in parables.

Then Jesus said, "So, Peter, you need to go to the shore with your fishing pole and toss out a cast. Reel in the first fish that bites. Once you've removed the hook, open the fish's mouth, and take the coin you find there, to pay our taxes—yours and mine."

I stood stupefied. Jesus wants me to catch a fish with a coin in its mouth and use that coin to pay his taxes?

Jesus almost giggled when he waved me away. "You'd better get going, so you can pay that tax, today."

Once my feet came unglued from the floor I wondered, how does he know these things? Jesus must know about my encounter with the tax man. But how? It had happened barely five minutes ago. No one could have gotten here fast enough to tell him about it.

And why couldn't we just wait for Judas to get back and pay the tax out of the wallet he keeps with our travel money?

Besides that, what was this talk about kids of rulers not paying taxes? All parents paid their kids' taxes—if the children were even taxed.

And then, I paused. Not long ago, I had confessed to Jesus that I believed him to be the son of God. Was he saying that, as the son of God, he owed nothing to cover the religious activities everybody else paid taxes to support? Was he saying God covered his tax portion? Is that why his tax payment was to be provided from God's creation and not our resources?

Jesus smiled at me. Did he know what I was thinking? It wouldn't be the first time.

I grinned sheepishly and turned to go. "I'll be back, soon," I said.

But I couldn't stop wondering. Maybe I was reading too much into it, but Jesus had clearly said the coin in the fish's mouth would be enough to pay our taxes—mine, as well as his. *Why was God paying my taxes, too?*

I wasn't a son of God—at least not in the same way Jesus was. I was a sinful fisherman and unworthy of such high status.

Besides, I had money to pay my own taxes. I wasn't without means.

Then, I thought of Jesus's instructions for catching the fish. Were the instructions significant, too?

If so, I realized I had to believe Jesus's unusual command and follow through on his instructions or I would never catch the fish, find the coin, and have my tax paid with his. These three things seemed to be important: *believing, obeying, and trusting the payment of my debt with Jesus's payment.*

I felt these things should mean something, but the significance eluded me. Maybe, Jesus would explain it when I returned, or maybe, I would grasp it better with time.

For now, I enjoyed the thought that God considered me worthy to pay my tax with his son's tax.

When I got to the shore, I put the hook into the water. I had never found a coin in a fish's mouth. This would be a first. And I wondered how long it might take for this particular fish to come along. Jesus had implied that I would be paying the tax, today, but sometimes my crew and I have fished all day and caught nothing.

In fact, that's what happened the day I left fishing to follow Jesus.

James, John, my brother Andrew, and I sat on shore cleaning our nets after a fishless night. As we worked, a great crowd of people came along the beach. I recognized the man in the lead as the new itinerant preacher and healer: Jesus. When he reached us, Jesus climbed into my boat. He asked me to move out from the shore so he could teach without being suffocated by everyone. I obliged. I wanted to hear him speak, and, this way, I would have a front-row seat.

Once Jesus began to speak, I could see why the crowds followed him. His teachings were nothing like the long, dry discourses of the religious elite who spat dust from brittle, old law books.

When Jesus finished teaching, he stayed in the boat and sent the crowd away. The people headed back to the parking lot near the pier, and I figured Jesus would climb out and go his way, too. But instead, Jesus settled in and said, "Climb in, and take us out deeper."

I shrugged and pulled the cleaned nets off the beach. I stashed them aboard before I set sail for our joyride.

Then after a few minutes, Jesus said, "Toss the nets out, here,"

I stifled a laugh. How do you tell a non-fisherman that fishing isn't that simple? I politely said we had just cleaned up from having caught nothing during the night. And I showed him the sonar fish finder screen: not a fish in sight in this spot. It wasn't a good day for fishing.

Jesus smiled, however, and he stood there waiting for me to let down the nets.

Finally, I gave in. "Sure," I said, "whatever you want." I nonchalantly tossed the net over the side of the boat. And before my hands left the net, I felt a tug.

I looked down to see swarms of fish jumping into my net. Yes, fish were jumping into my net! And they kept coming! And the boat listed from the lop-sided weight.

"Help!" I roared to my colleagues. "Hurry! Get the other boat over here! My net's starting to tear."

My friends' eyes popped at my bulging net, and they scrambled to bring the other boat opposite to even out the weight of the catch. We filled both boats to the rail with fish—more than we had ever caught at one time. Our cannery would be busy for weeks. We celebrated our success.

And then I remembered Jesus. Without him, we would be empty-handed. Jesus had been responsible for our miraculous catch.

I stopped work and said to Jesus, "Sir! I'm sorry I questioned you. You must, indeed, be a man from God, and I, a sinner, am not worthy to have you on my boat."

After the shore crew came to transport the fish to the cannery, I and my fishing mates thanked Jesus, again. And we remained in awe of what had happened.

That's why, when Jesus invited us to follow him, we accepted. He told us, "I will make you fishers of men."

And we have been following him, ever since.

And that's how I've come to be here, at his command, drowning a sad bit of bait in a few feet of water.

And because the water is clear and calm, I see a large fish circling the bait and starting to mouth it. Once I feel the line jerk, I set the hook and reel him in. I mustn't lose this fish. Jesus said the first fish would be the one with the coin. If he gets away, I'll never hear the end of it.

When I get it on shore, I see it's a nice-looking fish—perfect for supper—and I remove the hook. But I leave him lying on the sand.

I don't want to doubt, but I have to give myself a minute. I breathe.

Finally, I open the fish's mouth. And, even though I know the coin will be there, I shout when I see it!

In my exuberance, I look around for someone to share with, but there is no one on the beach. The coin glints in the sun, and I turn it over in my hand. It's exactly what Jesus said it would be—a coin in the amount of tax for two people.

Fileting the fish takes only a minute, and I throw it into the ice bucket in my trunk. Now, I struggle to stay within the speed limit on the way to town. I'm sure the cars I pass think I'm high on something because I keep shouting, "Thank you, God! Thank you for paying my taxes!"

I park and run into the crowded tax collection office. There, in front of everybody, I triumphantly slap the coin onto the clerk's desk. "For me and for Jesus," I announce loudly.

The tax officer doesn't look up. I know he hoped we would default and he could turn us in for nonpayment. I obnoxiously rub in my timely payment, several times, and even draw a smiley face next to my signature on the form. The clerk clenches his jaw, hands me my receipt, and then pretends I'm already gone.

On the way home, I belt out, "Glory, glory, hallelujah!" and envision our tasty fish supper. I can't wait for the chance to tell my story when we all get together, again. It will make the other eleven check with Jesus to see if I'm telling the truth, and I know Jesus will laugh. It will be his big, booming laugh!

I smile as I pull into the drive. There's no one like Jesus. And I renew my vow to always serve and take care of him. I've already committed to watch out for him, even though it seems he's always watching out for me.

Thank you, God, for allowing me, a poor bumbling fisherman, to serve your son. And thank you, again, for paying my taxes.

8
CRUMBS

I heard cries in the dark and knew Joyless was reliving her nightmare. If only I could, I would spare her from it and banish the memories. She had been doing better since we had escaped and come to our new country. But there was much from which to be healed.

In the slums of our old country, Joyless had suffered the misfortune to be born a girl and to be the youngest of seven children. Poverty and opium addiction by her father had determined her fate. The other children, one girl and five boys, had already been indentured to work miles away in the opium fields. By agreement, their employers sent a meagre sum of money home, but Fang needed more for his habit and to keep a roof over our heads. I did my best to shelter Joyless from him, but from the beginning, Fang groomed her for sale.

At first, Joyless would cry when Fang would drop her off at a hotel or someone's home. And she would be inconsolable when he picked her up and brought her back for me to tend. I did what I could to give her real love, but I could do nothing to free her or bring back her innocence. She became listless—a beautiful little girl with a deadness in her eyes and a lack of emotions. Like a little robot, she rose to do Fang's bidding and returned home to sit in a corner facing the wall. And I cried even though she didn't.

And then, one day, Joyless snarled at Fang when he ordered her to go with a man who had come to the house. She slashed at her father with her fingernails and her teeth, and she bit the man who had already paid his money. The sounds that came from her were not human; they could not have been produced by a young girl's vocal chords. Fang backed away and grabbed a broom, the only weapon he could find. But Joyless beat it out of his hands and pursued him out the door.

The frightened customer left without his refund—no doubt he would later find Fang and demand it. And Fang tried to follow the man, saying it was a mistake and that the girl would be fine in a few minutes. "She just hasn't eaten lunch, yet," he whined as an excuse. But the customer never looked back.

When Fang returned to the house, he grabbed a pitchfork, and I feared he would kill his daughter. "You have humiliated me!" he roared as he charged through the door. But Joyless was ready for him. With superhuman strength, she lunged and tore the pitchfork from his hands. Before I could stop her, she had pinned his shoulder with it to the door. His screams brought neighbors running. And Joyless defied them all. With a broom as her weapon, she glared through narrow slits, daring anyone to touch her.

The look on my daughter's face blazed wild and deadly. Although she wouldn't let anyone near her, she did let the neighbors pull the pitchfork out of the door and out of Fang. And she growled as they carried the injured man away. After they left, I shut the door, so that only Joyless and I remained inside.

In the dark room, with no windows or electricity, I felt my way to a candle on the table and lit a single flame. It cast enough light to see Joyless still standing in her defensive pose, frozen like a statue.

Even though my hands shook, I moved calmly to reheat soup over a small coal burner. As non-threateningly as possible, I laid two places at the table and sat to eat. I said quietly, "The soup is getting cold."

At first, Joyless did not move. But then, from the corner of my eye, I saw her drop the straw end of the broom to the floor. A moment later, she let the handle fall away, too, and she drifted to the chair. She sat, with her hands in her lap. I put soup into her bowl and turned back to finish my own.

Joyless sat oblivious to the food, but then her hand came up, and she picked up the spoon. Without moving her gaze from a blank spot on the wall, she moved the soup, back and forth, to her mouth.

When I cleared the table, Joyless remained rooted to her chair. I helped her up and into her bedroom where I laid her down. Then I closed the bedroom door and returned to straighten up the kitchen.

I wondered where the neighbors had taken Fang. Probably, to the city clinic, a mile away. I didn't want to leave Joyless, and I had to assume Fang was being cared for and didn't need me. I went to bed and fell into a fitful sleep. I could hear Joyless engaged in another battle in her dreams.

Three days later, my stiff and bandaged husband returned home. A neighbor assisted him and told me Fang had been lucky. The clinic doctor said it could have been much worse. Nothing vital was pierced.

At first, Fang refused to speak. He clenched his jaw and stared at the door of the bedroom where Joyless slept. I feared what he might do. But he did nothing. I think he realized he was no match for the girl in his present condition. But I could tell he wouldn't let the matter lie.

I fed Joyless in her room, to keep the two of them apart. But I knew it couldn't last. Fang improved, but his disposition did not. I feared he would kill our daughter.

I was almost right. He did the next best thing: he sold her—not for an hour or a night, but completely. Fang had gone out and returned home with the news: "Get her out of bed. I want her ready to go when her new owner arrives."

I cried and begged him to let her stay, and when he beat me and told me to do what he said, Joyless heard it and roused. She threw open the bedroom door and sprang from the room like a wildcat. She landed on Fang and tore at him. He had no defense and nothing to grab. I did my best to pull Joyless off him, and Fang crawled to the door and screamed for help.

The same neighbor who had brought him back from the clinic, pulled Fang into the yard, while I pushed Joyless back inside the house. Joyless fell into a kitchen chair and panted. While she sat, I went into action. I raced through the house throwing things into a couple of bags. Then I grabbed Joyless by the hand and led her out the back door.

I had no plan of where to go, but I knew we had to get away. Fang would be back, any minute.

Joyless followed without question. And, before long, we were down by the wharves. I don't know what I expected, because we had no money, but I raced to one of the cargo ships ready to pull away.

A man, onboard, looked at us and laughed. "Where do you think you're going?" And I said boldly, "We have passage booked on this ship. Let us aboard."

The man laughed again. "I don't think so," he said. "Where are your tickets?"

But a smaller man whispered in his ear, and the taller man changed his tune.

"Sure," he said with a leer. "Come aboard. I think we can arrange something."

Before I could think, Joyless pulled me onto the ship and asked the tall man where we could sleep. He led us to a small closet, and before he turned around, Joyless pulled me inside and latched the door. The cubicle was dark and smelled of wet mops. But we could hear the ship's horn, and we knew it was leaving port. Destination, unknown.

Hours, later, the man returned. In a surprising gesture, he opened the door and tossed in a sack of food. Then he pulled the door shut, again, and we heard him walking away.

We ate in the dark and in the knowledge that we were on our way to somewhere. We could feel the roll of the ship as it cut through the waves.

Several hours later, the man and his smaller friend returned. They came inside, closed the door behind them, and flicked on a flashlight.

Out of nowhere, a knife appeared in Joyless' hand. She held the blade against the tall man's neck. "If he touches my mother or me, I'll kill you," she said in a hard, deep whisper. The smaller man blinked and backed toward the door. "Now, now, kitten," he said. "No need to get violent. I meant no harm. I don't want any trouble."

The tall man spoke, too, "Hey, I don't want any trouble, either, little girl. We just wanted to help you pay your way, you know?"

Joyless growled, "I've paid enough in my life, and I'm not paying any more. If you want to kick us off the ship, you go right ahead. But I suspect you won't say a thing, because you weren't supposed to let us on board, in the first place, were you?"

The men knew she was right. And she let the two of them leave the closet.

I expected them to return, any moment, and turn us over to the ship's authorities. But it never happened.

We had a flashlight, now, and that meant we could watch the passage of time on my watch. We could also mark off the days.

After two days, we felt the ship dock, and we heard movement outside the door. We assumed the crew was going ashore.

Should we try to sneak out? I wondered. I was reaching for the handle when the door flew open and two large bags were tossed into the closet. A whisper explained that we were to get inside the bags. "They're laundry bags," the voice said. "We'll collect you soon and take 'the laundry' ashore." Then the voice was gone.

"I guess we have to trust them," I whispered, and Joyless climbed into her bag. I was afraid. What if this was just a way to dispose of us? I imagined the bags being knotted and tossed overboard. And then I decided that it didn't matter. We had no money and would likely starve, wherever we landed. I was half-starved, now. We hadn't eaten in two days.

In a short time, the door opened, again. And, this time, we were lifted out of the closet. I felt myself slung over someone's shoulder. I assumed Joyless was slung over another shoulder, and we were moving. Every so often, we bumped into something, and I had to catch myself to keep from crying out.

Now, the noises changed, and it sounded as if we had left the ship and entered a street. As our carriers walked, the sounds of voices grew fainter. I felt my bag lowered to the ground. The top opened, and the voice said, "You can get out, now."

When I climbed out of the bag, I discovered that Joyless and I were in an alley. And next to our bags was a small bag of food. But the men who had brought us here were gone.

And that is how we came to be in a strange city, in a new country.

I wanted to scurry off and see where we were, but Joyless stopped me. "We need to eat, first," she said, and I marveled at her calm. She was right. We needed our strength for whatever was out there.

After we ate, we hid the laundry bags; they carried the ship's markings, and we didn't want anyone to think we had stolen them. Then we left the alley and walked onto a downtrodden street. If this was a typical port town, the area nearest the wharf was the most rundown. I didn't feel safe, here, and I urged Joyless to keep walking in what I hoped was a better direction.

It took a half hour before we saw the city rise before us. When I spied a large hotel, I had an idea. We entered, and I asked the desk clerk where to apply for housekeeping. We followed where the young man's finger pointed, and we were soon filling out forms. I made sure Joyless listed her age as higher so she could work, too. "She's just small for her age," I explained to the clerk.

"How soon can you begin work?" the woman in charge asked us. And when we said we could start right away, she smiled. "Good!" she said. "I'll have Rebecca give you your training."

We spent the afternoon learning what the hotel expected from us. And then we were told to come back, tomorrow, at eight. Our interviewer walked us to the door with a smile and said goodnight.

What now? I wondered. *The sun is setting. Where are we going to sleep?*

As luck would have it, we passed a young couple with a tiny baby and overheard them checking their watches. "We need to hurry to get to the shelter before they close the doors for the night," the woman said. "We can't let the baby sleep on the street."

I nodded to Joyless, who nodded back. We gathered there was a homeless shelter nearby, and we followed the young couple to its doors. The couple was recognized and welcomed, and we were stopped, so we could provide information and learn the rules of staying there. It was straightforward and simple, and we were assigned two cots in a small dormitory for women. Men had their own space, in another part of the facility. I cried when I saw the showers. We hadn't been able to wash for days. It felt wonderful to be clean and to rinse out our clothes.

A soup supper nourished us before bed, and a roll and coffee got us going early enough in the morning to get to the hotel by eight.

Our assignment allowed Joyless and me to work together. So, we cleaned each day, and at the end of the week, we received a paycheck. It was my first! Fang had always kept every penny of our money.

We came every night to the shelter to sleep and to eat breakfast and supper. And, now, we had a few dollars for lunch. On our days off, we explored the shops around the hotel and the shelter, and we picked up a few things we needed.

Joyless remained a quiet girl. Except for her dreams, she looked to be more at peace, here, than I had ever seen her.

And then on one of our days off, we watched a young woman race across the street and into the arms of a young man. They kissed, and he twirled her around and set her before him with love in his eyes. It made me smile. But it affected Joyless in a completely different way. I turned to find her pulled back against the building and drawn into a ball on the sidewalk.

I bent over her. "What's wrong, honey?" I asked. She didn't respond. Joyless had gone inside herself and become the child I had known, back home. And although I sobbed over her, she did not recover. I half-carried her to the shelter. There, the woman in charge expressed concern. "Let me get someone to look at her," she suggested kindly. "We have a counselor, who is very good with these sorts of things."

The counselor spoke quietly to Joyless and asked me what I thought had caused the breakdown. I hesitated, at first, but I decided to tell her our entire story. Her eyes grew saddened, and she set a daily time to meet with us. I reported to the hotel that Joyless was sick, and I was relieved when they sent their best wishes and said they hoped she would be back soon.

Joyless made progress with the counselor, but her dreams still haunted her. Then, one day, after she had returned to work, a young man noticed her and complimented her. Without warning, a deep, low growl poured out of her that frightened the young man—and me. The man backed away and disappeared. Joyless continued to stand there, panting like an animal, and I rushed her into an empty room until she returned to normal again.

This was the second time I had heard this voice from her. It wasn't her voice, and it worried me. I remembered hearing wives' tales of demons who took over people's souls, but I had never thought it real. Now, I believed Joyless had a demon hiding inside her, and I didn't know what to do to rid her of it. I avoided telling the counselor because I had always heard that people with demons were locked up and never heard from again. I couldn't bear that happening to my poor girl. She had been through enough in her life. I hated that her demon had followed her all the way here.

I feared we could lose our jobs if the demon showed itself at the hotel. And I feared the shelter might ban us. Joyless often growled in her sleep. But others had nightmares, too, and, so far, the shelter had been understanding.

Around this time, I saw in local news a report of a healer named Jesus, who would be in town for a week. The reporter interviewed someone who had been healed. They said, "I came from another country to find Jesus. He had healed the skin cancer of a friend, and I didn't want to miss a chance for my healing, too. I had to wait in line, but it was worth it! Jesus touched and healed all of us. I was even close enough to see Jesus cast demons out of a little boy."

Demons? Did that man say demons? I listened more intently, but the reporter scoffed at the mention of demons. "I can't believe demons exist," the reporter said. "Isn't it more likely the boy had a mental illness?"

But the healed man insisted, "There *are* demons. In my country, demons cause people all kinds of harm. And there are only a few true exorcists. Most who claim to be exorcists are only fakes. They cheat people out of their money. But this Jesus is for real! All of us waiting in line for healing heard the demons cry out when Jesus ordered them to leave the boy. And the child was instantly freed of them. You would believe it, too, if you had seen the difference in the boy!"

The reporter interviewed others, and I waited to see if he would share where to find Jesus. But he mentioned nothing.

I was consumed, now, with finding Jesus, and I asked everyone if they knew where he might be. No one did, until Lily, a girl from the shelter, whispered she had seen him secretly enter a big house, a couple of blocks away. "I think he's staying there," she confided.

Beat still, my heart! Was this my chance? Could I take Joyless to see Jesus at that house? I didn't want to expose her to large crowds or reveal her illness, unnecessarily. Meeting Jesus at the house would be perfect.

I convinced Lily that I needed to see Jesus early the next morning, and I rose early and dressed.

But my plan didn't work out as I had envisioned. Joyless had growled most of the night in her dreams and I was too afraid to awaken her early. But I was also afraid to leave her. She might awaken and need me to calm her.

What should I do? If I waited too long, I might miss Jesus.

I finally decided to go without Joyless, and I would try to convince Jesus to come to the shelter. He wasn't that far away, and surely, once he heard the need, he would come, wouldn't he?

Lily led me to the house, and I gathered my courage to knock on the door. I wasn't sure what I would say when someone answered, but the words poured out of me: "I need to see Jesus. It is very important. Is he still here? Please don't turn me away."

The man at the door sighed. He muttered, "The poor man gets no peace." Then he shut the door; but I had the impression he went to ask if Jesus would see me. Lily and I waited. After a minute the man reappeared, and he let us into the house. He took us to a room where another man sat eating his breakfast. Lily nodded that this was Jesus. Because I still feared being tossed out, I hurried forward and fell on my knees at his feet, and I blurted out my plea for him to drive the demon from my daughter.

I don't know what I expected, but I heard him say, "You're not from here, are you?"

Of course, my accent had given me away.

But I felt it was more than that. I felt he knew all about my illegal arrival aboard the ship. And I became afraid.

And then he said in my native language and without a smile, "You do realize, don't you, that I'm here to serve the children of *this* country. There are many, here, for me to take care of before others are served."

He paused and buttered a piece of toast. Then, he held it up and said, "It's not right to take the children's bread and toss it to the dogs."

I winced. People from my old neighborhood had been called *dogs* by those who had more money and prestige. But I swallowed my pride and bowed my head to the floor. I pled my case. "Yes, sir," I replied, "but even the pets under the table eat the children's crumbs."

There was a long silence, and I feared I had offended him. Tears spilled onto the floor beneath me.

But then, I heard a kind voice, one that encouraged me to look up. Jesus was smiling, and I smiled back. His eyes reflected kindness, and they held my gaze. And he said, gently, "For such a reply, your request is granted. You may go; the demon has left your daughter."

I kissed Jesus's feet and backed away. I had never petitioned such a gracious person. And my heart beat wildly in expectation of what he had said. I had come hoping he would come to the shelter to touch my daughter. And I had hoped he truly had the power to heal. And now he tells me my daughter has been healed, without his physical touch. Such a thing is unheard of! And yet, I believe him. I feel it in my soul. I saw it in his eyes. I sense that he is a man of God—a God I barely know. And I believe he can do anything!

I make myself take time to thank him, but I want to hurry back to the shelter. I leave him to finish his breakfast, and I charge out the door. Lily and I race down the streets.

I tear through the front door of the shelter and down the hallway, startling several people along the way. And I find Joyless still sleeping. And I don't awaken her. I kneel beside her face and watch her sleep. And I already know my answer.

Her closed eyelids are not jumping and her brows are not furrowed. A slight smile plays over her lips. And I hear a girlish giggle in her sleep. And while I watch, she smiles again, yawns, and opens her eyes.

"Good morning, Mother," she says. "I love you!" And I sob. My little girl has never, ever said she loved me. I feel her hug, and I nearly squeeze the stuffing out of her.

"I had the most beautiful dream," Joyless said. "I dreamed we were in a big house, and a nice man was eating his breakfast, and he smiled at me. I've never known such a nice man."

I rocked Joyless in my arms, and I said through my tears, "His name is Jesus."

And she said, "Jesus. I'm glad to know his name. He's wonderful, isn't he?"

And I could only whisper, "More than wonderful!"

The morning sun streamed in the windows of the shelter more brightly than ever. I think it's because it's a brand-new day—the first day my daughter has started to live.

Instead of *Joyless*, my girl has become *Joyful*. And she laughs and teases and rejoices in the smallest things. Her heart has become kind and light and loving. And she is more beautiful than ever.

She befriended Lily, who had taken me to Jesus, and the three of us have gone several times to hear Jesus speak in nearby towns. And Joyful blew him a kiss, one day, as he passed by. Jesus grinned and "caught it" in his hands. He put it in his pocket, and Joyful laughed.

Our laughter turned to mourning when we heard Jesus had been killed. But we all rejoiced at the news that he had risen to life, again. In fact, we were among those who got to see him alive! And we continue to celebrate that he is the son of God and will come again, one day, to heal the entire world of evil and hurt.

Until that day, life goes on under his blessing and with his spirit.

My favorite blessing came four years ago when a dear young man who is also a follower of Jesus became my son-in-law. I have four beautiful grandchildren, who are being raised in the protection of God's love and the beauty of his healing grace.

One day, I hope to find my other children and free them, as well, by the grace of God. I know that, in Jesus, all things are possible.

9

ALL I OWN

Winter had been long, so I wasn't surprised people had thronged to be outdoors. But I marveled that so many people had packed the fairground stands to listen to an itinerant preacher.

I'd never heard of this guy, Jesus, and wouldn't have bothered to come, except my housekeeper claimed he had turned water into wine at a wedding. A parlor trick, I sniffed, except that Nathan confirmed her story. Nathan, one of my colleagues, had been at the same wedding.

I arrived late on purpose to avoid sitting through the whole thing. Jesus had been speaking since one o'clock this afternoon, and it was now nearly three.

The only seats left were at the top.

As I huffed and puffed in my climb, I checked out the audience. What was it about this man that drew them? It wasn't his looks; in his blue jeans and T-shirt he might have been anyone from the crowd. Nor was it his delivery. He was neither flamboyant nor loud. I had expected the carnival barker or the hypnotic backwoods preacher. But Jesus was neither. He never raised his voice.

"Stop judging others," Jesus was saying. And he offered the example of a man with a log in his eye trying to remove a speck from his friend's eye. It was such ridiculous hyperbole that everyone smiled. "Don't be foolish," Jesus said. "Get rid of the log in your own eye before you attempt to pick the speck from someone else's eye."

He's got a pithy message (pun intended), I supposed. *But there was nothing earth-shattering in it. This must be a simple crowd.*

Once I dropped into my seat, I heard him say, "Choose your path through life carefully. There's only one way into God's kingdom. Most people choose the tall gate and the wide road where they find company and ease of travel. They ignore the little sign that says the wide way leads only to hell. Be careful. Read the fine print and look for the narrow road. Follow it, because it's the only road to life."

Interesting, I mused. But his next words jarred me. I recognized them as a barb against my colleagues in the religious leadership. Jesus said: "Watch out for false teachers in sheep's clothing, who are wolves bent on satisfying themselves at your expense. They look real, but they are not. They speak about God, but they don't know God or how to guide people to his kingdom. You'll find them forcing their way to the front of the line on judgment day, recounting how well they've kept the laws and served their congregations. But I'll reply: 'I never knew you or authorized you to do any of the things you are bragging about. Leave me and go back to your useless labors.'"

So, I decided, *this is his game. Jesus is a rabble-rouser, who claims a special standing with God the religious establishment doesn't have.* I should have stood, right then, to denounce him, but I couldn't get my breath or leave my seat. My legs had turned to jelly from the climb to the top of the bleachers. I could only cross my arms and huff as I listened to more of his diatribe.

Back home, I stewed throughout the night and into the next day.

After breakfast, Traci, my housekeeper, waved her feather duster, so I took my coffee to the patio. Traci answered the ring of her phone, and I heard her say, "Yes, after we left the fairgrounds, several of us followed Jesus's bus to a nursing home where Jesus healed several residents. Two women leaped from their wheelchairs and danced a jig. A twisted man unfolded and raised his arms in praise to heaven. A mother, who had been guiding a soft drink straw for her vacant-faced son, screamed when the young man pushed himself from his seat and wrapped his arms around her. The young man had fried his brain on drugs and been consigned for life to the nursing home. And, now, he was healed!"

Oh, brother! I scoffed. *Is the world going crazy? How do these people know this wasn't a setup? It's just too 'neat' to be anything else.*

I fumed as Traci ended the call with instructions to reach this afternoon's meeting place. This Jesus thing was getting out of hand. Besides, healings are a sore subject with me. My son was born with crippling spina bifida, and his mother died in childbirth. I'd heard whispers that I must have committed some secret sin for which God was punishing me. But I knew better. I was upright and clean. I had done nothing wrong that wasn't confessed and accounted for before God. And since that is what God demanded, the fault could not be mine. Perhaps it had been my father's, or even my wife's sin. I would never know.

By birth, I was part of the local religious leadership, and I taught and served as a righteous example to others. God had further blessed me with inherited wealth. And even though I was the youngest on the worship council, I was every bit as respected as those who had served for decades.

When I arrived at today's council meeting, a heated discussion was underway about Jesus. Maury Strobe had risen to his feet and spat, "We must do something to stop this charlatan! He claims to be God and able to forgive sins! Then, to ratify his claims, he pretends to heal people."

"And he bad-mouths us!" I hurried to contribute. "I've heard him, myself."

The council members turned to stare at me.

"You went to one of his meetings?" Maury asked, in astonishment. "I hope no one saw you and assumes you are in agreement with him!"

I hadn't considered that, and I quickly defended myself. "I didn't go to support the man; I went to get first-hand proof of his evil ways."

When I repeated what I had overheard at the fairgrounds and from my housekeeper's phone conversation, the council members threw up their hands. "See!" said Maury. "This man is dangerous."

We stewed for an hour over what to do but we could not come up with a plan. Because of Jesus's popularity, we needed to be very careful. We decided that, for now, we should attend Jesus's meetings and challenge Jesus with questions designed to expose him. I judged it a good plan, and I couldn't wait to do my part.

My first chance to confront Jesus didn't come for a few weeks. Jesus had been preaching away from our locale, and I could only vent my frustration at the television screen as I watched reports of his activities. I could see the size of the crowds swell, day by day. Reports said people were calling in sick to their jobs so they could caravan to Jesus. I knew it was true because my housekeeper didn't show up one week. When Traci came back from her "sick" leave, I caught her talking in the hallway with my son's live-in caregiver.

Traci said to Marsha, "I wish we could convince Mr. Zeller to take Jason to Jesus. I'm convinced Jesus could heal him!"

I burst into the room and shouted, "Nobody is taking my son anywhere near that quack! Don't you have dusting to do, Traci Allen?"

Traci scampered out of the room, and Marsha replied, "Of course, Mr. Zeller."

I doubted Jason had overheard any of it. He was supposed to be down for his rest. But I was wrong.

"Dad," Jason said to me that night, "can I ask you something?"

"Certainly, son," I said. "What's up?"

Jason squirmed, as only a nine-year-old can do—even one confined to a wheelchair with spina bifida. "What would it hurt if Traci and Marsha were to take me to Jesus? If Jesus could help me, it would be great. Really wonderful, you know? But if he couldn't, well, it wouldn't hurt things more than they are right now, would it?"

My heart constricted. My poor boy! I would move heaven and earth to be able to bring him healing. And now he was doubting my intentions. I closed my eyes and sighed.

Jason hurried to reassure me. "It's okay, Dad," he insisted. He wheeled himself over and placed a hand on my arm. "I understand if you think it's not a good idea."

His words twisted in my gut. My Jason worried more for my feelings than for himself.

"I love you, Son," I whispered. "And I would do anything for you. I just need to think on this, okay?"

That night, I couldn't sleep. Arguments occupied my thoughts. *What if Jesus COULD heal Jason and I never let him try? I would regret it the rest of my days. But how could I give this man a chance to disappoint my son? I couldn't live with that, either.*

Plus, I was a council member. I had a responsibility to uphold the teachings of Scripture. What message would I be sending to people if I took Jason to receive a healing? The crowds would think I endorsed the preacher and believed his powers were from God. No, I couldn't go to Jesus.

Then, another thought intruded: *What better way to expose the man's quackery than to demonstrate his inability to heal my son? It would be a powerful proof to the crowds, and it would exonerate me before the council. I could lay it before the healer as a challenge.*

But it was too dangerous. I would be using my son as a pawn in an uncertain scheme. Various scenarios stormed through my mind.

Could I prepare Jason to expect nothing? Was he mature enough to understand what was at stake? How could I be certain he would understand? If he didn't, my lesson would be cruel. Perhaps if Jason were older, I could be sure he wouldn't be hurt. But Jason was still cocooned in the dreamy-eyed innocence of youth.

Then, I wondered, *was I sheltering Jason too much? Would this be a powerful lesson for my son about deceitful people who spread false teachings? Was this challenge indeed the best way to expose the charlatan?*

I argued the pros and cons for days, even after Jesus had left town. I had much to lose. But I could not let it go.

Then, when I thought I had finally pushed it out of my mind for good, Jesus came back to town.

Actually, Jesus stayed in a little village outside of town and people flocked to him, there. For two days our streets lay deserted, and the mall and supermarket parking lots sat empty.

But Traci showed up to clean. I pretended I had expected her, and I hid behind my newspaper and drank a second cup of coffee.

Marsha exclaimed in surprise, too. "Aren't you going to hear Jesus?" she asked.

"Kevin and I will go after I'm done," Traci replied.

And then, because I could overhear, they returned to their work.

Neither woman could have known the struggle playing out in my heart. One minute, I imagined myself asking Traci where to take Jason this afternoon. And, the next, I was scolding her for being so gullible about Jesus. One minute, I envisioned myself advising Marsha to pack Jason's traveling gear. And, the next, I was ignoring Jason's unrepeated request for us to see if Jesus had the power to heal him.

When Traci was packing her cleaning supplies to leave, I could stand it no longer. I tossed down the newspaper and jumped from my chair. I marched into Jason's room and sat down next to him. He and Marsha looked up from his homework.

"Jason," I began, "I'm going to treat you as an adult for a few minutes. Is that all right?"

Jason cocked his head and said, "Sure, Dad."

I stalled Marsha, who had risen to give us privacy. "Please stay," I told her. And Marsha sat.

"Son," I said, "because I'm on the council, it's important I not endorse anyone who's not teaching the right things about God and religion. Do you understand?"

Jason smiled. "Yeah. You can't let people think you believe in Jesus."

I chuckled. My son was smarter than I knew. "Right," I said. "But I want to take you to him. If Jesus truly is a healer and can help you, it would be wonderful. But…"

Jason interrupted. "But," Jason said, "if he's not, and he can't help me, it will help you show people they shouldn't follow him. Right?"

I had sold my son short. Jason understood well what was at stake. "Right," I said. "So, do we go?"

Jason reached out for a hug, and I let my tears come.

Marsha was already tossing things into Jason's travel pack.

I had forgotten about Traci until Jason yelled into the other room: "Traci! Are you still here? We're going to see Jesus!"

A thump on the kitchen floor told me Traci had dropped her bag of supplies and was running to the bedroom. She burst through the door. "Yes!" she called out, and she and Marsha danced around the room.

In mock grumpiness, I said, "Well, if we're going, we'd better get to it!"

The ladies giggled, and I snagged the car keys from the peg in the kitchen. With instructions from Traci to guide us, Jason, Marsha, and I headed for the village. Traci headed home to pick up Kevin.

I feared we'd never get to Jesus through the crowd. But Marsha began to bawl, "Coming through with a sick person, here!" And when people saw Jason's wheelchair, the way parted before us.

Then I caught whispers of "that's the councilman, isn't it? And is that his boy?" I ignored the comments and pressed onward. Within a few dozen feet of Jesus, we joined a mass of people on crutches, in wheelchairs, or with white canes. A young couple held a bandaged baby, a white-haired man limped on a prosthetic leg, and a group of determined teenagers supported a friend so emaciated a stiff wind might blow him away.

Jesus was speaking, but I was too busy imagining which of the scenarios of healing/not healing would play out for my son. I wished, with my whole heart, that Jesus was for real and Jason would walk away from this place whole.

What I hadn't seen on the outskirts of the crowd were Maury Strobe and Simon Doyle from the council, but they had seen me. Fortunately, they were too far away to intercept or call out to me. I'm not sure what I would have done if they had. Everything in me was focused on the improbable-but-yet-hopeful exchange between Jesus and my son.

When Jesus stopped speaking, I strained to see what prompted sporadic outbursts of cheering and clapping. Had the healings begun? Under different circumstances, I might have lifted Jason to tell us what was happening. But hoisting him up would give the wrong signal if Jesus proved to be a huckster.

I had expected to intercept and maybe question the healed when they returned. But, apparently, they left in a different direction than they had come. We didn't encounter them. I supposed the crowd opened on the other side of Jesus to let the miracles pass.

Miracles. I had said it. I was here to confirm or deny the possibility of *miracles*—especially at the hand of this man.

What was a miracle, anyway, but a confirmation of God's interest in the affairs of his people?

Miracles by the prophets of old had served to prove God's power and protection of his people. Miracles helped Moses get Pharaoh's attention. The miracle of the sun standing still swayed a battle in Joshua's favor. A miraculous shutting of the mouths of lions had proven God was with Daniel. And Elijah had called miracle-fire from heaven to declare God's superiority over Baal.

As our line dwindled—with purported healings of blindness, deafness, muteness, and broken bones—I found myself praying, *God of all power and love, you know how often I have prayed for a miracle for my son. Today, I pray it again. I do not doubt your ability to heal or your purposes if you do not. I ask you to help me and my son to be strong if this man is not your emissary as he claims to be. But, O Lord, if he is operating under your authority, I pray that, today, my son might be healed!*

Grasping for faith, I scrutinized each healing we were able to observe. The nature of the maladies left them open to doubt. Was the mute girl truly unable to speak? Could the deaf child truly not hear? Was the blind man truly blind? Because I did not know the people, I couldn't tell if they had feigned their sickness as part of an elaborate scheme.

Perhaps the last candidate would help me decide. The only person ahead of us, now, looked to be truly sick. I could not imagine that he wasn't.

Friends of the emaciated young man laid him at Jesus's feet and backed away. I saw that Jason watched closely, transfixed.

My heart feared. If Jesus failed with this young man, what would I do?

I weighed every outcome of the scene before me, frame by frame, as in slow motion.

The sick young man smiled up at Jesus and Jesus smiled kindly back at him.

"Do you want to be healed?" Jesus asked. And the young man nodded his head.

"Do you believe God loves you and can heal you?" Jesus asked, next. And the young man's smile never wavered.

Jesus nodded, lifted one hand in prayer, and placed the other on the thin shoulder.

"Father," Jesus prayed, "bring wholeness to this child of yours, today." Jesus remained as he was, with eyes closed.

I watched intently. Was there trickery, here? Was the young man not truly sick? But even as I questioned, I knew the answer. The teen was too thin and too sickly for this to be a scam. But would he be healed?

At first, nothing changed. The crowd was silent, and I stopped breathing.

And then, I detected a sign.

The young man's pallor disappeared in a rush of healthy pink that flushed his cheeks. Then it spread to his neck, across his back and chest, down his arms, and, finally, to his legs and feet. With the flush of color came a perceptible fleshing out of his muscle and tissue. My eyes widened when he hurried to unfasten the top button of his blue jeans; he was filling out quickly, and his pants had grown too tight for comfort! I laughed. And then, I cried. The sickly, thin teenager stood whole and well before us. And we were next.

Emotionally exhausted, I found myself unable to move. It was Marsha who stepped up to push Jason forward. I could scarcely breathe. My plan to challenge Jesus with my son's healing had dissolved in the face of an undisputed miracle.

Jason was so expectant I ached for him. Jesus reached out for his hand, and Jason lifted it eagerly.

"I've always wanted to meet you," Jason said.

I chuckled through my tears when Jesus said, "And I've been waiting to meet you!"

Jason now looked up and said, "You're going to heal me, aren't you?" Jesus simply said, "Yes."

As he continued to hold Jason's hand, Jesus said, "Pray with me, okay?" And Jason bowed his head.

Jesus prayed so quietly that only Jason, Marsha, and I could hear him.

"Father," he said, "I pray this boy's healing might be proof to many that you are with me and that you hear me. Thank you, Father, that you are the source of all goodness and healing."

The words of Jesus's prayer flowed deep into my being. I had never heard anyone pray to God as their father. And although I was steeped in the doctrine that God was *one*, I wondered at the idea of a man with a kinship to God that transcended humanity.

And I noted that Jesus had specifically prayed for Jason's healing to be an example. How could Jesus have known my intent? Would Jason be healed?

Jason's head remained bowed, and I could still see the twisted curvature of his spine in the wheelchair. For just a second, I panicked. It wasn't going to happen.

But even as that doubt entered my mind, I began to see change. Instead of starting from the top down, as it had with the teenager, the change in Jason began with his feet. His toes turned out in a way I had never seen them. And then Jason began to bounce his heels as his legs grew strong. Soon, he was swaying in his seat, like Ray Charles at the piano. And I sobbed as I watched his back straighten and support him as it had never done. By the time the healing reached Jason's arms and shoulders, he was standing and clapping his hands in the air.

And Marsha and I danced with him before his healer! I began to chant Psalm 103, the Psalm I had always loved for praise:

> *"Bless the Lord, O my soul, and all that is within me, bless his holy name."*

As I shouted out each verse, the crowd joined with me. Their voices soared on favorite passages, such as:

> *"He has not dealt with us according to our sins, nor rewarded us according to our iniquities. For as the heavens are high above the earth, so great is his mercy toward those that fear him."*

I felt a heady surge in my soul as we ended with:

> *"The Lord has prepared his throne in the heavens, and his kingdom rules over all.*
> *"Bless the Lord, all his angels, that excel in strength, that do his commandments, and that hearken to the voice of his word.*
> *"Bless ye the Lord, all ye his hosts, ye ministers of his, that do his pleasure.*

"*Bless the Lord, all his works in all places of his
dominion;*
"*Bless the Lord, O my soul.*"

Jason and I embraced for the first time on four feet. And I knelt before Jesus. "Thank you!" I wept. "Thank you!"

Now, Jesus's associates guided us to the opening in the crowd. We floated through the mass of the people. I still worshipped with every fiber of my being.

Then, I stopped, short.

At the back of the crowd stood Maury and Simon. The frowns on their faces could not have been deeper. And they stood rigidly straight in their judgment.

I clung to my son and passed them by, without a word.

Although Jason was now well, I kept Marsha on staff to tutor him and help him catch up in schoolwork. In the fall, Jason would join classmates in a public classroom—a prospect that excited him. And Traci sang through the house as she cleaned. Although she and Kevin had been at the back of the crowd (where we would have been had it not been for Marsha's calls to let Jason's wheelchair pass), they had believed Jason would be healed. When news had traveled back through the crowd that a councilman's son had been healed, Traci and Kevin had sung Psalm 103 with us.

I could not have been happier, but I can't say everything was now perfect in our lives. I was all but shunned by the council. When I attended our first meeting after the miracle—*yes, it was a miracle, wasn't it?* — I expected a chance to validate the miracle. But I was met with hostility and closed-mindedness by men I had always respected and admired. Did they not believe Jason's miracle was proof of God's hand? Could they not consider Jesus to be God's messenger? I made my arguments, but no one responded.

Maury never spoke to me again. He didn't even look in my direction during the meeting. Simon seemed embarrassed and also ignored me. The only one who acknowledged me was Nathan, the one who had seen the water turned to wine. Nathan proposed quietly that no one could do the things Jesus did unless God was with them. But Maury swiftly countered with, "He could also be doing them by the power of the devil!"

I thought, *that doesn't make sense! The devil does evil, not good things. And how could my Jason's healing be evil?*

I left the meeting with my thoughts in turmoil. Perhaps I needed to gather and bring more evidence to the members. I would spend more time listening to Jesus and evaluating what he said.

Nathan cautioned me this was risky, but I refused to accept that no matter how much proof I might bring them, the council would not listen.

Over the next days and weeks, I hung around the edges of the crowds surrounding Jesus, and I absorbed his teachings. Now that Jesus had proven himself by healing Jason, I listened with new ears when he said such things as:

- "If you have wronged someone, make it right with them before you come to worship God."
- "Don't make swearing oaths a habit. It is not in your power to uphold them, especially oaths sworn before God."
- "Don't avenge evils done to you. God will avenge what is needful. Instead, love your enemies and pray for them. After all, that's how God has treated you."
- "Spend less time in worry. God knows your needs and will supply them more generously than he provides for the birds and the flowers. You are much more important to him than they are."
- "You have been taught to hate your enemies, but I tell you to love your enemies and do good to them. Be perfect as your heavenly father is perfect."

Each of these teachings came from Scripture I had memorized from childhood, but Jesus more accurately reflected their righteous intent than what I had been taught. I recalled Deuteronomy 15:7-11 about personal relationships and God. I remembered Leviticus 19:12 and Deuteronomy 23:23 about oaths. I recalled Leviticus 4:20; 19:28 and Proverbs 25:8-10 about revenge. I pondered Psalms 23 about God's provision. And I remembered Micah 6:8, to do justice, but love mercy, and to walk humbly before our God. Jesus's lessons stirred me to find the living principles at the heart of the old teachings. Where I had been taught to hate evil and condemn evil-doers, Jesus walked me further: to love God and offer his mercy and redemption to sinners.

And then, one day, Jesus shared something so unusual about the kingdom of heaven and eternal life it bewildered me. He said unless one's righteousness exceeded that of the religious leaders and teachers they would not enter the kingdom of heaven.

Did that include me? As a religious leader, I had taken an oath dedicating myself to observing every law. No one lived more righteously than I did. Plus, my lineage guaranteed me a place in heaven as Abraham's child and a religious leader who observed the law.

And yet, I knew I was not perfect. No matter how I strove to be righteous before God, I could not control my every thought and impulse, and I was never sure I had confessed and made purification for every sin. But I was more righteous than ninety-five percent of the people on earth.

How could Jesus say my most careful righteousness was not enough to save me? Was heaven—the kingdom of God—an empty place?

But, in other lessons, Jesus taught that if we would seek the kingdom, we would find it.

Between these two messages, how could I be sure I had inherited the eternal kingdom life? I needed an explanation.

I knew Jesus would be leaving our area, any minute, to head for the capital. Everyone, including me, would be there for the annual religious celebration. And I knew it would be impossible to get near Jesus in the city. The capital would be packed with celebrants from across the country and around the world. If I intended to pose my question, I had to do it now.

I apologized for rudely pressing past everyone leaving the stadium. But I dared not stop. Even with my haste, I nearly missed him.

I saw Jesus's associates boarding the bus, and I panicked. *Please don't leave!* I breathed. And I ran!

People stared, but I didn't care. Out of breath, I knelt before Jesus by the bus door. He smiled, and I had the distinct impression he had been expecting me—maybe even delaying until I had come.

I blurted, "Jesus, good teacher, what do I need to do to inherit eternal life?"

Jesus looked at me and asked, "Why do you call me 'good?' Isn't it true that no one is 'good,' except for God?"

I stammered. I wasn't prepared for his question. What was he implying? Did he think I was calling him God? Nothing could be further from the truth. He should have known that, with my background, I would never call any man God. I would never veer from the bedrock truth of Deuteronomy 6:4: *"Hear, O hear: The Lord our God is one Lord."*

Then Jesus said, "You know the commandments: do not commit adultery; do not kill; do not steal; do not bear false witness; defraud not; honor they father and mother."

I replied quickly, "Of course. I have kept them all since my youth."

Now Jesus said, "There is only one thing left to do. To have treasure in heaven, go, sell everything you possess and give it to the poor. Then, come, take up your cross, and follow me."

His words left me speechless! What kind of teaching was this? Before I could recover and ask for clarification, Jesus boarded the bus. I stood dumbly as the vehicle moved past me and turned onto the frontage road. In less than a minute, Jesus was gone.

My mind whirled. I had expected a great teaching on holiness, not a call to poverty. Why had I never heard him give this advice to anyone else in his messages? Was this instruction unique to me? Was he saying I was letting my wealth stand between me and God?

I couldn't imagine such a thing. I tithed and gave to the poor as the law required. Did he truly mean for me to give up everything—one-hundred percent—of my money and belongings? How would that bring me eternal life? Wasn't wealth a sign of blessing from God?

As I reflected more, I decided that Jesus's reply did sound like a few of his other teachings. In many lessons, he would reference existing law and then extend it to the *nth* degree to make a point about the law's intent. In one example, he said if your eye caused you to sin, you should pluck it out, because it was better to lose one eye than to have your entire body thrown into hell. No one would take that literally! It was meant to make a point. It was hyperbole—over the top. So, perhaps Jesus was telling me to give more of my wealth to God. Not necessarily *everything*, but *more*. I could do that. I *would* do that.

But somehow, this interpretation did not satisfy me. What did an increase in my giving have to do with me achieving eternal life? Would I ever understand?

The high religious festival in the capital was the pinnacle event of the year for thousands of people. My soul swelled to be part of what seemed like the entire world honoring God. And this year, for the first time, Jason would walk the parade route to the meeting hall with me and sit in the capital council meetings. As my son, he had that right.

We parked in our hotel lot and left on foot to take in the festival sights. At the sound of shouts, we leaned out to look down the street. Perhaps the high council leader was arriving.

We watched as hands in the distance flew up, like the stadium wave at a ballgame, to honor the one passing. And we heard shouts of "Hosanna! Save us now! Blessed is he who comes in the name of the Lord!"

I found the shouts unusual and recognized them as the praise our ancestor David had composed in Psalm 118:25-26 in reference to the coming of God's promised world leader. I wondered who was being lauded in this way. In a few more minutes, I would see.

Imagine my surprise when I discovered Jesus, perched above the seats of a shiny, new convertible, speckled with confetti and ticker tape. Hundreds of people around us turned to snap selfies on their phones to immortalize the moment.

The scene troubled me. I found it ironic that the people hailed Jesus as God's messiah, while the council insisted he was from the devil. I struggled with both points of view.

"He waved to me!" Jason cried out, and his yell brought me back to the reality that this man had healed my son. He was no devil.

The parade ended at the steps of the impressive council headquarters, and Jesus left his vehicle to climb the steps. Jason and I were swept along by the surge of celebrants in his wake, and we were soon inside the building, too. But we were nowhere near Jesus. We stood, trapped in a crush of people, unable to move from our spot until later in the day.

We missed that Jesus had created a ruckus, overturning tables in the council lobby. I shook my head. Didn't Jesus understand how unpopular he was making himself with the religious leadership?

I also missed a heated exchange between Jesus and various council members where Jesus deftly deflected questions designed to derail him. I recalled the strategy of our local council to try to trap him, and I guessed that the capital high council had attempted something similar, only to find that Jesus turned every question back on the questioner. Jesus then engaged in his infamous parables, each thinly denouncing the council. I cringed. Why did he go head-to-head with the leadership, right here in their headquarters, the locus of their power? I feared for his life. So did my friend and fellow council member, Nathan.

"He's either naïve, or he has a plan of protection we haven't seen," Nathan said. "I fear it's the former. I heard Jesus yell a disturbing cry over the city. He said, 'How I would have gathered you as a hen gathers her chicks, but you would not allow it. And so, your house is left empty and desolate. Sadly, you will not see me, again, until the day you say, "blessed is he who comes in the name of the Lord."'"

Nathan and I agreed that Jesus's cry didn't sound like a conquering messiah.

That evening, the city calmed as each family prepared the customary ceremonial dinner. We could not know that, while we were preparing our food and hearts for repentance and worship, another scene, a hideous scene, was playing out in the chambers of the council—a council that was supposed to be closing for the required preparation. I thank God we didn't know and that we weren't there. And I'm thankful Jason was shielded from what we learned, later, was a rushed illegal prosecution and public execution of Jesus. When we learned of it the next morning, we were warned by Nathan to draw our blinds so we couldn't see, even dimly, the deadly scene playing out on a distant hill. We didn't want Jason to see his healer dying.

Evidently, God didn't want to watch, either, because, mid-afternoon, God closed his eyes!

For three hours, darkness blotted the sun from sky. It was more than a cloud cover; it was an inky blackness, darker than night. The earth quaked, and the entire city fell to its knees in dread. Everyone prayed it would end, which it did.

That night, Nathan came to us with the report that the darkness had begun the moment Jesus had died.

Nathan had kept a low profile and had been able to follow the activity of the prosecution and execution. He told how his stomach had churned at the false charges and murderous call for Jesus's blood.

"Once the council got their way and Jesus was condemned," Nathan said, "several council members paraded around the execution site to make sure nothing went wrong. When it grew dark and the ground trembled, they fled like rabbits back to the headquarters. Stumbling in the darkness, they lit candles in the inner chambers and cried out to God for forgiveness 'on behalf of the people.' What a laugh! But God would not be mocked. No sooner had they bent their knees than the massive tapestry, overhead, dividing the public from the private worship area of the inner chamber ripped with a horrendous roaring tear from the ceiling to the floor! The torn tapestry pieces fell in a great heap, and what had always been the chamber's secret and exclusive domain of God, lay exposed. In fact, when sunlight once again returned, a shaft of light shot through an outer doorway and down the chamber hall, to illuminate, for the first time, the secret place that no unauthorized eyes had ever seen."

"It was a sign of God's displeasure!" Nathan fervently announced. "God's servant had been killed by the council, and God was showing the murderers they couldn't hide!" I agreed with Nathan's interpretation at the time. But later, he and I understood differently: we came to view the torn tapestry as a sign of the completion of God's saving work—of opening the way of righteousness for sinners to access his presence.

"Nathan?" I asked. "Is Jesus truly dead? It's hard to believe!"

Nathan nodded sadly.

Jason cried out, "It's wrong! Jesus was from God! He healed me, when no one else could do it. It was evil to kill him. I hate the council for what they've done!"

I agreed, but I dared not say so. It was wrong to say evil of the council. And it was wrong to hate. Jesus, himself, had said so. He had said, "Love your enemies," and I had regarded it as a lofty sentiment. But now I wondered, *how does one love enemies who kill you?* I sought to comfort my son as he wept.

Long after Jason went to bed, Nathan and I talked. We discussed our future.

"I can't return to the council," I told my friend. "I don't see things the way I used to. And I can no longer be a part of the religious duplicity I feel among the members. Even when I proved Jesus was not a charlatan, they refused to consider he might be from God. And now they shun me and my son. It is not easy to walk away, but I can't continue as before."

Nathan said, "Caleb Zeller, my friend, I need to tell you what I am doing. I also am convinced the council is wrong. And I fear their evil is not finished. Because of that, I am helping to hide Jesus's associates. I fear for their lives once the festival ends. I fear that even you and Jason may be in danger if the council decides to pursue those who have been healed or have been sympathetic to Jesus and his cause."

I could see Nathan's point. I needed to protect myself and my son.

But it surprised me that Nathan was harboring Jesus's friends. Although admirable, it was dangerous. When Nathan left, I prayed for his safety and the safety of those he protected.

Because of the restrictions of the annual celebration, no one left the capital until Sunday. Our packed belongings sat by the door, ready to load into the car.

Unexpectedly, Nathan showed up, breathless, at our door.

"You can't go, yet!" Nathan puffed. "I have news you need to hear. He's not dead!"

"He's not dead," Nathan repeated. "Jesus is alive!"

Before I could wrap my thoughts around the idea, Jason jumped up. "Is he truly alive?" he asked.

I choked back my alarm. How could this be real? Jason was in for a crushing disappointment. I hoped I wouldn't have to ask Nathan to leave.

"Nathan," I said, as calmly as possible. "You're not making sense."

Nathan nodded and said, "I know. But it's true!" Then he smiled broadly. "It doesn't make sense, but I've seen him!"

In exasperation I threw my hands in the air.

"Nathan, you told us on Friday that Jesus was dead. And now you say he is alive. Which story is true?"

Maddeningly, Nathan giggled and said, "Both."

"They can't both be true," I argued angrily, but Nathan stood his ground.

"Come and see," he invited eagerly. "Come and see what I have seen. Plus, you'll meet the others who have seen him, too."

Then Nathan said, "Don't reason it out. Just come with me—because of our friendship."

It seemed too much for him to expect of me. But I saw Jason's eyes pleading. "Can't we go, Dad? Can't we go and check it out?" he asked.

I wanted to trust Nathan, but this fantasy was impossible. Someone was playing a trick. How could I dissuade Nathan and bring him and Jason back to reality? Would it help if I went?

"Wouldn't we be in danger?" I asked.

Nathan replied, "With so many people milling around, today, and leaving for home, we shouldn't attract undue attention. I'll help carry your luggage. It'll take only a few minutes in your car."

Jason studied my face, and when I sighed, he knew we were going.

"Yes!" Jason cried. "I'll get my suitcase."

I had wondered where, in the city, one could hide a host of Jesus-followers; so, I was not surprised when Nathan guided us to the other side of the city. Behind a tall high-rise, we left our luggage in the car. Inside the building, we boarded an elevator to the top floor, and partway down the hall, Nathan knocked on a door that opened into a large suite.

I recognized those inside as Jesus's associates. But there were others, too—perhaps twenty to thirty people.

Nathan introduced us, and we were offered seats and coffee.

Before I could advise a soft drink for my son, Jason insisted on coffee, too. So, I ordered lots of cream and sugar. My son was growing up. Allowing Jason coffee, at this juncture, was a small concession, to encourage him in the company of men.

Nathan asked Peter to tell us what had happened earlier in the morning, and I sat in disbelief at his tale of finding Jesus's tomb empty and abandoned by the guards. Women who had gone to the tomb before Peter, insisted Jesus had appeared and spoken to them.

I shook my head. It had been a mistake for me to come and bring Jason here. I considered how to leave, gracefully. This group had somehow become deluded.

But then, another man called out his story. Everyone listened.

"My friend and I are from Emmaus," he said. "We had been here in hiding for three days and then planned to return home. Before we left, we heard the stories of the empty tomb from Peter and the women, and we wondered what their discovery meant. We pondered it as we traveled.

"As you know, traffic on the main highway is always backed up after the festival, and we remarked on a stranger, on foot, who was passing us by. We laughed when he asked to hitch a ride. He had been making better time than we had in our vehicle.

"Although we still moved at a crawl, we minded the pace less with our amiable passenger. We discussed the news of Jesus's death and the rumors of seeing him alive. And the stranger contributed by quoting Scripture prophecies foretelling the death and resurrection of God's messiah. He brought to mind things we had not considered. We asked him to stay for supper once we got home, so we could talk more.

"He accepted, and we sat down to eat. In a mannerly gesture he offered to say the table grace, and we bowed our heads. All seemed normal, until we heard his prayer. Then, in a flash of insight we realized who he was! We saw the nail prints in his upraised hands, and we heard him address his prayer to his father. And after the amen, he vanished!"

"Vanished?" I asked. "How did he vanish?"

"He simply disappeared. It was like he dissolved into thin air," the man said.

I shivered and whispered, "A ghost! Surely, it was a ghost! Dead men do not rise from the grave and appear and disappear."

A quiet voice to my left said, "But dead men do rise from the grave."

Nathan made the introduction: "Caleb and Jason, meet Lazarus."

I stared. I had heard the story of Jesus raising a man named Lazarus from the dead. But I had dismissed it.

Lazarus said, "One minute, I was dead, and, the next, a voice called to me. I felt compelled to respond. In the darkness, and breathing in the stench of death, I struggled to sit and then move toward the faintest of lights. Finally, I felt the sun, and I heard gasps and cries. Fingers removed the gauze from my eyes, and I saw Jesus's face. I wept. I knew I had been restored to life! And I treasured the warmth of hugs with my sisters and friends.

"I was—and am—no ghost," Lazarus said. "As you can see (touch me, if you like), I am flesh and blood."

My mind refused his story. This was impossible. It was insanity to believe such things. Surely this man was mistaken about his death. I needed to leave this place before I, too, lost my sense of reality. And I had to get Jason away from these men.

As I looked for a way of escape, I felt a breeze sweep through the room.

It could not have come from the windows or any door. I peered, again, at every possible exit and found everything closed and locked.

Then, I caught the startled expressions on the faces of those around me. With mouths open, they stared at something behind me. I turned—just as Jason turned—and I heard my son scream, "Jesus!"

In astonishment, I beheld him! The man who had healed my son was here, standing behind me in this very room. Jason ran and clung to him and cried, "I knew it must be true! I knew you were alive!"

My legs gave way, and I dropped to my knees. If this was a delusion it was more than realistic. There were even nail holes in his feet!

Was this real? Or was it a ghost? I could not decide.

It took the touch of Jesus on my shoulder and his hand on my chin to lift my eyes to his, to shake my doubts.

"I am real, Caleb," Jesus said with a smile.

And then Jesus did one more thing: he dipped a piece of bread into my coffee cup and put it to his lips. I saw him take it in and swallow. All of my learning had said ghosts do not eat.

Now, Jesus patted Jason on the head and released him. Still on my knees, I hugged my son, and I looked up to his healer with grateful tears. And the words I had thought I would never repeat formed on my lips: "My Lord and my God!"

And in that instant, Jesus vanished.

How could I ever leave this place? I wondered. *How could I ever leave these people who have shared this wonder?*

We sat and talked late into the night. Even Jason stayed awake, to absorb every word.

"We need to make plans," Peter said.

"But what are we to do?" asked Bartholomew. "Where are we to go?"

Nathan suggested, "Stay here, for a while. Perhaps things will settle, and it will become safer to move around. Besides, I believe Jesus will appear, again, and give more direction."

"That sounds reasonable," I suggested. "If Jesus has appeared three times, it's logical to assume he will appear again."

"I hope so," Matthew said. "Thomas needs to see him."

"What will we do for food and supplies?" Nathanael asked.

Philip laughed, "Always the practical one!" And the others laughed, too.

"But he's right," said Matthew. "If we're staying, we need provisions. There are a couple dozens of us, now, and our numbers could grow."

Nathan quieted them. "I will continue to be a go-between. I can get you food and other necessities. You needn't worry."

Everyone nodded. Nathan had already proven his helpfulness. So far, he drew no suspicion.

In the middle of the discussion, I heard my son ask, "Could Dad and I stay here?"

I smiled. My wise son knew we belonged here.

We stayed. And Jesus did reappear and taught the things we all needed to know so we could follow through on the work he had begun.

After a month, Jesus bid a final goodbye and returned to his father in heaven. We would remain in the world and receive his holy spirit to help us.

As time passed, I arranged with an accountant to sell my home. Jason and I needed it, no longer.

The day the accountant brought my money, I recalled Jesus's puzzling words: *"Sell everything you possess and give it to the poor, and then you will have treasure in heaven. Do that and come; take up your cross and follow me."*

I understood it, now, and I did as he had instructed. I had followed, and now I spread my wealth before our group of friends and said to use it wherever needed. Others also sold land and homes, and no one in our group went without the things they needed.

Matthew often recited Jesus's words: *"Seek first the kingdom of God and his righteousness, and all you need will be credited to you."*

And I treasured the knowledge that Jesus had opened the way for everyone—including me—to have eternal life through his sacrifice for our sins. The laws I had always followed could never save. They could only point to the day when the blood of Jesus Christ, the son of God, was offered to cover our sins. Jesus's resurrection proved his victory over sin and death. And the curtain once separating sinners like me from the holy presence of God was torn away, forever.

Through Jesus, our future has no end. We trust the promise that one day Jesus will come again, to set up his perfect rule. Then, as prophesied, there will be peace throughout the earth. In the meantime, I give all my heart, my mind, my soul, and my strength to follow wherever Jesus leads.

His path has already given me Jason, whole and eager to serve with me. And Jesus has healed my unbelief. My treasure now lies above, not in things below. All praise to Jesus, our savior and our God!

10

MERCY

The minute she pulled her credit card from her purse, I had it on my reader. And my scanner got her driver's license. And she had no idea!

I patted myself on the back; I still experienced a high whenever I fleeced a mark. After supper, I tapped Melinda Cordray's stolen information into my computer and hacked into her email account. The hack was vital for checking her Web history and logging into her online banking account with a change of password. I even stayed up most of the night to get her insurance and hospital records. When you knew what you were doing, it wasn't hard. It just took patience and a few well-placed keystrokes.

I didn't know Melinda, but it didn't matter. Once I assumed her digital identity, I cleaned out her bank account. Then I had my purchases on her credit card shipped to one of those commercial postal boxes signed out in her name, too. With her money, I paid off my last surgical bill, and, now, with her insurance, I'm considering getting my knee done.

It's all such fun. And I've grown bolder with every theft, over the years. People I work with would marvel at the technical expertise I've developed in carrying out my schemes.

And it might interest them that my life of cyber-crime began because of an article in a technical magazine at our office. As a lark, I tried out what I learned, just to see if it worked. Like the people I cheated, I had had no idea how easily one could glean personal and financial details from the internet. When you added an internet hack to what you could swipe from somebody's billfold with a wireless radio-frequency magnetic strip reader, you had everything you needed.

I knew only one other person who did what I do. But he also caused havoc with car computers and home alarm systems. I steered clear of that stuff. I didn't want to get caught or get somebody killed. I just wanted their money. The only tricky part to my scheme was using the stolen insurance. I had to change Melinda's hospital records to Mel Cordray, a male, and show *my* blood type and prescriptions and not hers. I suppose it could happen that Melinda might have an accident requiring emergency surgery and they would give her the wrong blood in a transfusion, but it was unlikely.

Melinda might not discover her loss for a while—until she tried to pay for gas or a few groceries with her credit card. *Poor thing!*

But I didn't feel too bad. Insurance covered everything, and Melinda's bank and credit card company would reimburse her, soon. The medical card discrepancies weren't likely to show up for as much as a year. Melinda was in good health, and she had just completed her annual checkup.

Nope. I imagined Melinda would enjoy a good night's sleep, tonight. And I would sleep well, too.

In the morning, I shaved, ate breakfast, and went to work as *Duane Barton*, my given identity. And there, my paranoia kicked in. I checked my bank account, first thing. I figured if I was robbing unsuspecting people, someone out there might be robbing me, too.

But everything in my online statement looked fine, and I got on with the business of the day: writing software games for my employer's company.

After work, I visited my new commercial postal box at the mall— the one I held in M. Cordray's name.

"Sorry, Mr. Cordray," said the clerk who peered through the back of the box at me. "I couldn't get everything in here. If you come to the door, I'll bring your items around."

I smiled. Then I ad-libbed, "I found a great catalog and didn't realize how much I had ordered."

The clerk pushed six cardboard boxes through the door. "Yes, it looks like you went on a pretty big spending spree!" he said.

I made four trips to the car with my loot and wished the clerk a good day. I couldn't wait to get home and unpack everything. Great stuff: high-end countertop appliances for the kitchen (I like to cook), a newer I-Pad, a laser-printer, a leather jacket, and a pair of Italian shoes. People at my office thought I had a rich uncle who sent presents all the time. This stuff should bring lots of oohs and ahs!

Plus, I had extra bucks to take Lucy to a fancy place for dinner. I called her, and we met at The Hanover. Lucy took it for granted that I had money. And she didn't complain. She surprised me sometimes, though—like this evening.

"I wonder if you'd go with me to hear a speaker, tomorrow night," she said. "Betty says he's remarkable. She insists he often heals people from the audience. I thought we might check him out."

I shrugged a *why not* and said, "Sure. Let's do it. What time should I pick you up?"

A healer, huh? I figured it would be entertaining to guess how he did it. Probably had several plants in the audience. I chuckled. *A cyber-thief going to check out a huckster. It was ironic.*

The next night, we drove to an outdoor amphitheater. I was surprised at the size of the crowd. We weren't down front even though I had flashed a healthy sum of money to encourage people to give up their seats. This guy must be good.

The first four rows were filled with "disabled" persons of one sort or another. They appeared convincing, I thought. I did wonder what the charlatan would do with the young microcephalic in the second row. That would be a tough one to put over. I would be using my opera glasses on that one!

Lucy left her seat to say hello to friends. "From my worship group," she said. I was impressed with the number of people she knew. When someone came to test the microphone on stage, Lucy hurried back to her seat.

"I'm excited," she said. "A friend, here, is hoping one of her patients will be healed."

I raised my eyebrows but said nothing. Lucy would find out, soon enough, that this was a sham.

A man named Peter introduced the speaker as "Jesus," and an ordinary-looking man crossed the stage. The crowd cheered. I guessed they had heard him speak before. This whole setup intrigued me.

But Jesus's voice and delivery were common. And I didn't understand his words.

"Blessed are the poor in spirit; for theirs is the kingdom of Heaven," he said. *"Blessed are they that mourn; for they shall be comforted. Blessed are the meek; for they shall inherit the earth…"*

My attention strayed. I tried to keep up, but his words swirled in my head without landing on anything.

Then, when he began to talk about adultery and lust, I thought, "Aha! Finally, something I can relate to." But I was wrong.

The guy was an extremist. I scoffed when he claimed that if a man so much as "looked on a woman with lust" he had "committed adultery with her, already, in his heart." I thought, *Not quite!* but I must have said it out loud because Lucy looked at me strangely. After that, I made a concentrated effort to keep my thoughts to myself.

Jesus droned on about loving your enemies and doing your charity-giving in private. He even expounded on praying and fasting. And all the while, I fidgeted in my seat.

Then, for no discernible reason, his next words burned their way into my brain:

"Don't store up treasures on earth where they are vulnerable to rust or moths or thievery. Instead, set your heart on things that last. Store up treasures in heaven."

It wasn't just his words but how he said them. Somehow, he knew heaven from first-hand experience. And, although I was twenty rows above and yards away, his eyes locked onto mine, and he spoke directly to me: he knew I was a thief!

I heard little else for the rest of the afternoon. And until people clapped I didn't realize he had finished.

Everyone surged to the front to meet him, but he was whisked off the stage by several large men. What mayhem!

The unruly crowd milled around and murmured when they couldn't find him, and they blocked in the disabled people in the front rows.

"He didn't heal anyone," Lucy said in disappointment. "The pushy crowd made it impossible. I feel sorry for my friend, up front."

I was disappointed, too. Jesus's healings were the reason I had come. How odd that a huckster healer wouldn't have healed anyone.

The amphitheater slowly emptied. Lucy and I let the disabled rows leave ahead of us.

Then, on the way to our car, someone shouted, "Jesus is at the park!" Immediately, the cars ahead of us jockeyed to merge into the egress and down the hill to the park.

Was it logical to assume that Jesus might conduct his healings at the park?

The cars ahead of us held the disabled from the amphitheater, so we were the last to arrive. Others had been at the park for fifteen minutes.

Lucy and I ran toward the cheers and shouts. By the time we could see the action, three disabled individuals remained in line. I was glad we hadn't missed the whole show.

I watched a twisted old man stand straight and toss his cane into the crowd with a "Whoopee! Praise God!" Then, a little girl who was supposedly deaf looked into Jesus's face as he placed his hands over her ears. After a prayer, Jesus whispered in the girl's ear. Her eyes lit up, and she jabbered something to her mother. (*How touching!* I thought.) But I still had my doubts.

My eyes now fixed on the last person waiting for healing: the microcephalic I had noticed in the amphitheater. *So,* I thought, *I haven't missed it. This should be good!*

Jesus spoke to the deformed young man, but I couldn't hear what he said. Then, Jesus prayed. I kept my eyes open during the prayer, so I wouldn't miss a thing. I wondered how Jesus would let this kid down when he couldn't heal him.

As I expected, after the prayer, nothing happened. The boy's eyes stayed closed and his jaw hung open, as before. In fact, the boy's caregiver began pushing his wheelchair out of the way. But she stopped and stared.

The change started below the neck. Shoulders that had atrophied because the brain had never ordered them to work, now broadened to the correct size. And the torso filled in to match. That's when something dropped to the ground below the wheelchair. I marveled to see the caregiver pick up a feeding tube, no longer needed. Now, the boy's neck muscles bulged. And as I stared in disbelief—*how could this be?*—the boy's skull and cranium filled out, and he closed his jaw. His face took on a calm, intelligent air—so different from the staring, mentally challenged vacancy that had marked his visage since birth. The caregiver screamed and danced in joy. The boy's eyes filled with tears as he focused on his healer. His fingers reached out to touch Jesus's face. Without a word spoken, I knew the boy was saying thank you!

Jesus whispered in the boy's ear, and sheer delight blossomed on the young man's face. When the boy turned to wave goodbye to Jesus, my breath caught, because I hadn't noticed that his legs and feet had strengthened. He rose from his wheelchair and pushed it aside. Then he walked arm-in-arm with his caregiver through the onlookers.

Lucy hurried to catch up with him and dragged me after her.

"I'm so happy Ethan was healed!" Lucy called out to the caregiver. "I was praying the whole time!"

"So was I," replied the woman. "I wanted it to happen, so much!"

Ethan cried, "I feel tingly and wonderful all over!"

I stood mute. There was no way Jesus had faked this. I didn't know how, but Jesus had done the impossible.

I was hooked. I had to come to another meeting.

I never got to return to hear Jesus, however, because the next day, while I sat working at my desk, an officer of the government slapped handcuffs on my wrists. My cyber-crimes had been discovered.

Everyone expressed shock. No one believed I would have done such a thing. And the one I hated to disappoint most was Lucy. She's the only one who came to the capital city prison to visit me.

At first, all I did was weep.

"I can't tell you why I did it," I confessed, "except that I got caught up in the idea I could get away with it. Knowing how to worm my way into people's private stuff fed my ego and excited me. And before long, I had hacked the records and files of dozens of victims. It gave me a rush to sneak in and redirect their information and spend their money on myself. And I justified it by arguing that insurance would kick in and cover the losses."

Lucy listened as I condemned myself. She was the least sinful person I knew, and I made her my confessor. I was sure she would walk away, soon, and I wouldn't blame her.

When I had said all and run out of things to confess, Lucy and I talked about things we used to talk about before prison separated us. Lucy talked of her family and our friends—friends who were still her friends even if they were no longer mine. And she told me of going, again, to hear Jesus. In fact, she had gone several times.

"Jesus is getting himself into trouble," she said, one day. "Religious authorities show up at every event and try to trick him with questions on religion and government. He always turns the questions around and ties the authorities in knots. But this just makes them angrier. They're jealous of the attention he's getting. And he isn't kind to them in his teachings. He warns that the authorities don't represent God's word properly. And worse, Jesus claims to be God's son and the ruler of a heavenly kingdom. The religious authorities shout 'blasphemy!' and condemn him. I'm afraid for his life."

As I listened, I couldn't imagine the authorities killing a man who healed the unhealable and cut to the heart of living a godly life. But the subject disturbed Lucy, so unless she brought it up, I didn't discuss it.

Lucy and I also avoided talking about my sentence. At court, Melinda Cordray's eyes had burned me throughout the proceedings, and the prosecutor had called for the death penalty under a seldom-enacted punishment for thefts of over a certain amount of money. My take had amounted to several hundred dollars over the limit, and the judge had brought down the gavel.

To my lawyer's credit, he continues to plead for mercy as my deadline approaches. I can't say I haven't received justice—I believe I deserve my sentence—but I hope for mercy.

The hardest part of the wait is not knowing if a reprieve might come. But as the deadline draws near, I find I'm coming to peace with my sentence.

Lucy still cries, bless her heart. I regret failing her in every way.

"You'll find someone better than me," I tell her. "I'm ready to die. I know I did wrong, and I'm sorry. I've prayed for God to forgive me, even if my earthly judge does not. I pray that when I come into God's presence, I might find his mercy."

The night before my execution, Lucy and I say our goodbyes. "I can't bear it," Lucy cries. "You are always in my prayers. And I want you to remember that I love you."

I had wanted to be strong for her, but instead, her last remembrance of me is of a blubbering mess huddled in the corner.

I had wondered if my execution might be delayed because it fell during the annual religious festival. But no, the jailer has appeared at the moment he was supposed to come.

I am dry-eyed, now, and I follow him solemnly to the gate where another officer takes charge. I am put into a van and driven to the execution site. There, I sit and wait. I have learned two others are scheduled to die with me.

But it doesn't matter. Alone or with others, death is death.

I see a second van arrive, and another prisoner is brought to sit next to me. The man is surly, and he's covered in tattoos. I don't bother to strike up a conversation, and neither does he. We wait silently for the third person to arrive.

When he comes, the third condemned man doesn't arrive alone. A mob of people, led by a host of religious leaders, surges into the waiting area with him. I can't see him for the crowd, and when I do, I am stunned!

Lucy was right. The condemned man, at the center of the commotion, is Jesus. He looks like he's been through a war. Bloodied and bruised worse than an abused animal, he has a crown of thorns jammed onto his head.

When the officers unfurl a banner that mocks him as a king, I understand what the crown symbolizes. According to Lucy, Jesus had claimed to be the son of God and the ruler of a heavenly kingdom.

I marvel at the man. Even in this despicable state, he carries himself with dignity. I cringe when the government officers and religious authorities spit on him and punch him, but there's nothing I can do to stop it. I wouldn't treat a dog the way they're treating him. *The man's going to die—isn't that enough?* Even the surly, tattooed prisoner joins in the taunts.

I try to focus on the fact that it will be over, soon, for all of us.

When the officers prepare the execution, I can't push past the pain. It's a cruel death to die, and there's little respite. Although I want to die well, I cry out, repeatedly. The tattooed man also cries out and curses, but I notice that Jesus never speaks a word.

The hurt grows increasingly unbearable, and to make matters worse, a haughty group of religious authorities keeps parading past

Jesus with self-satisfied sneers. Jesus lifts his eyes to heaven, and I hear him pray, "Father, forgive them; for they know not what they do."

His words infuriate the religious actors, and they scream at him, "Don't you pray for US! You claim to be the son of God, but you're helpless to free yourself from this execution." They now play to a mob watching the events. "See!" the religious leaders call out. "He healed others, but he's powerless to save himself. If he is a king of heaven, let him show it and we will believe him. He claims he trusts in God; so, let God deliver him—if God will have him!" Everyone laughs, and the tattooed prisoner adds to their taunts by snarling, "Yeah! If you're the son of God, save us, too!"

And in that moment, my anger overcomes my pain. "Shut up, you fool!" I shout at the tattooed man. "We're getting what we deserve. But this man has done nothing wrong."

I realize I truly believe that. I agree with Lucy's assessment, that Jesus is being put to death because of jealousy. And even through my pain, three other truths burn inside of me. One is the memory of the day Jesus healed the microcephalic boy. Two is the prayer he has prayed moments ago when he called God his *father*. And three is his admonition to me at the amphitheater to "store up treasures in heaven where they will be safe." Somehow, these three things coalesce into a single truth for me: I believe Jesus is the son of God and the king of heaven! I don't understand why God is allowing him to die, but I still believe. I reason that Jesus has God's power, he has an intimate relationship with God, and he spoke of heaven to me as one who knows it well and gave me advice.

My inner eyes translate the scene before me from the apparent defeat of an ordinary man to the triumphal passage of a king to his kingdom. And I heed his admonition to "store up treasures in heaven" as a promise that I can lay up treasure there.

I am overcome with yearning to be in that kingdom. And I say to this man, who is dying with me but who knows heaven in a way the rest of us do not, "Lord, remember me when you come into your kingdom."

Jesus rests his eyes on me as he did in the amphitheater, and the one who promised healing to the microcephalic boy now promises me, "Truly, I say to you, before this day ends, you will be with me in paradise."

Instantly, I have peace! I know in the deepest part of my soul that I have been right—that I am in the presence of God's own son.

And although I still don't understand why he has to die, I do believe Jesus cannot stay dead. He will soon be alive in paradise. He has a kingdom to rule. And he has assured me I will see it, too. And I know that because of him I will soon walk into God's presence with mercy on my head and rejoicing on my lips.

11

FOR THE LOVE

Tired as she was, I knew Mama was kneeling beside her bed to pray. And I felt guilty because I knew the prayers were for me. Those prayers, offered night after night, had no doubt kept me alive.

It wasn't her fault I had turned to the gangs after my dad died. It was just that, like our neighbors, we had nothing. And the gang leaders and drug pushers had come into the 'hood flashing gold jewelry and expensive cars, and they had lured me and my friends to join them.

Even though I had never taken the drugs, I had sold them. And somehow, I had avoided jail. When I would bring the money home and tell Mama she didn't have to work anymore, she never said a word, but I knew she never spent it on herself. She put it away in a tin box at the back of her closet and pulled it out if there was a need among our friends or neighbors. In some small way, I think she felt it redeemed the money of its sinful past. Our rent and groceries came from her hard work cleaning houses.

I made few demands on her; I was never home except to sleep. And even then, I came in long after she retired.

When my dad died, I was ten. Dad had worked in maintenance for the poor excuse of a school in our neighborhood. He had been a good man. His death hit us hard. Mama let herself sob for a week, and then she packed up her emotions and let them out only after work on Fridays.

Cleaning houses. Tiring. But it paid the bills.

I heard Mama pray hundreds of times, "Please God, keep my Solly safe, and keep him away from drugs and crime. He is a good boy. Help him not to fall into the hero-worship of thugs and criminals. Help him see they are not the friends he thinks they are. Open his eyes to the truth and keep him for me."

Then she would pray for neighbors and friends who were sick or couldn't pay their utility bills. And she would ask God to show her ways to help them by providing soup, knitting socks, or sewing warm coats for their children. Her heart was as big as her ample bosom, and she spent a lot of time doing whatever she could.

When I awoke in the morning, Mama had left for work but I found breakfast laid out for me. I stuffed the cold sausage and coffee cake into my mouth and washed it down with cold coffee. I couldn't take time to reheat it in the microwave. Any minute I expected the sound of a car horn. Q'el had something for a few of us to do, and it wasn't good to be late.

Often, we had to back up Q'el's threat against someone who had crossed him. Our mere presence was enough to bring offenders around. And no matter how early we got to the Q House, there were always users waiting for us to hand out supplies. It disgusted me. What losers! Emaciated dregs of humanity, eager to shoot up or snort. I felt no remorse for feeding their habits. It was their doing, not mine. And if they wanted to spend their lives and their money this way, who was I to turn down the profit?

Day after day, it was the same. My friends and I ruled in our little world, and I looked for nothing more.

And then today happened. I shivered on the porch step even though my high-ticket jacket was more than adequate for the cool afternoon. I hugged my knees and rocked. When I heard Mama's footsteps, I made myself look up and act casual. It would frighten her to find me here at this time of day. She would expect the worst. Was I hurt? Was I in trouble?

When Mama saw me, surprise widened her eyes, but she caught

herself. She acted as if it was not unusual to find me here so early on a Friday. I admired her control. I knew she wanted to smother me with questions and gather me into her concern. But she said nothing and walked up the front steps with her bag of groceries. As she passed me, I muttered, "Lost my key."

"Uh-huh," she murmured. And she turned her key in the lock.

When she entered the apartment and set her bag in the kitchen, I slipped inside and closed the door. I stood in the hallway. I lived here, but I felt I needed permission to be here at this hour.

Mama never looked up but offered, "I've got leftover pot roast in the fridge, and I picked up a cherry pie."

I lifted my head and shuffled into the kitchen. Mama busied herself putting groceries away, and I know she heard the scrape of my chair across the linoleum as I sat. I wondered how long it would be before she would ask me what was wrong.

Supper heated on the stove, and Mama set dishes at our places. Then, as she always did, she bowed her head and gave thanks for the food. Before closing the prayer, she ventured: "And thank you, Lord, that my son can eat supper with me, today."

That's when the sob came. I could hold it in no longer. Mama looked up to see me weeping over my plate. And she came around the table.

"Solly, what's wrong?" she asked.

I couldn't answer. She put her work-worn hands on my shoulders and let me cry. It had been a long time since I had cried in her presence. I know she wished I was still her little boy with a skinned knee, and she could take me in her lap.

When I could manage it, I wiped my tears and threw myself back in my chair. I said, "It's Manny. Manny's dead."

I saw her legs wobble, and she returned to her chair at the table. Manny had been my best friend since kindergarten, and his mother was my mother's friend.

"What happened, boy?" she asked. I saw the fear in her eyes. Had it been a gun fight? Or a hit by another gang?

To me it was worse.

I blew my nose. "Bad drugs," I said, and I hung my head. "I can't believe it! Why did it have to be Manny?"

I knew what she was thinking. What a waste! Drugs permeated the lives of too many families on these streets. The drugs not only enslaved the users but often took their lives. I knew she hated them.

And then I grit my teeth and moaned, "I killed him, Mama. It was me! I gave Manny those drugs! I didn't know they were bad!"

Now, I knew she was angry, but I was angrier at myself. I beat my fists on the table and wept. Then I stood, knocking over the chair. I clawed at my pockets and pulled out several bills. I tore them into shreds. "I should die, too!" I cried. "What have I been doing? Oh, Manny! I'm sorry!" Then I staggered from the kitchen and threw myself onto the sofa.

Mama came to the living room and sat next to me until my sobs quieted. Then she got up and turned on the television. She made sure the program was not a news channel or a police episode. And she brought our dinners to the sofa. I did not eat, and she only picked at her meal. I saw nothing on the screen. My mind played and replayed Manny's death and my culpability.

I'm not sure when Mama left me to clean up the kitchen. And I didn't realize I had fallen asleep. When I awakened in the morning, still on the sofa, a light blanket covered me. A pillow and quilt on the recliner said Mama had not trusted my state of mind and had slept in the chair.

Before I sat up, I smelled coffee. My stomach rumbled. I hadn't eaten since lunch yesterday.

I devoured a cold breakfast and poured myself a hot coffee. Mama came down the stairs dressed with her hat and gloves for worship meeting. When I was a child, our whole family had gone to worship. But it had been years since I had gone.

Mama never said a word; I think she knew I wasn't ready. While she puttered around the kitchen in the few minutes before she had to leave, I took my coffee to the sofa and pretended to be absorbed in a cooking show, of all things. And she left me alone, no doubt praying I would not harm myself or disappear for who-knows-where before she returned.

At noon she pulled out a tray of cold fried chicken, a salad, and all-day beans, and I shared it with her. Then I returned to my spot on the sofa. Mama moved like a ghost around me, doing the things she always did on worship day: reading a book, listening to music, sipping lemonade. On worship day her sewing machine sat silent. A child's coat lay over the sewing chair almost finished, and I wondered which neighbor would receive the gift. The coat brought a new pang of guilt. I knew well that many of our neighbors were in more need than necessary because fathers and mothers had become addicted to the drugs the gang sold. Any jobs the people might have been able to find disappeared once a blood test informed their would-be employer. And I knew children suffered the most. I felt guilty because I had sold drugs and guilty because I hadn't cared how much they had hurt people—until now.

The afternoon dragged on, and I wallowed in my sorrow. That night I told Mama, "I've quit the gang."

She smiled. "I wondered," she said. "I'm glad."

"It's not all good, though," I said. "Q'el says I'd better stay out of his way, you know?"

Mama didn't know, but she understood how dangerous it was to quit the gang. "Stay safe," she said, and I nodded my head.

On Monday, I left the house. I needed a job; I would not live off my mother. Because there were few non-gang port jobs in the Joppa area and none that would hire me because I'd left the gang, I drove out further. By the end of the day, I was stocking supermarket shelves on this side of the capital city, in Emmaus.

My pay didn't compare with the drug money profits, but this was clean money and it helped pay my part of our household expenses. Mama accepted this money.

And because I worked afternoons, I helped Mama make her morning soup deliveries and clothing drop offs in the neighborhood. That's when I saw firsthand the damage the drugs had done in the lives of otherwise good but poor people. The saddest were women with many children who had lost their husbands. And it haunted me. I couldn't wait for the afternoons to come so I could escape to work, away from all the messed-up families.

I observed that people who lived closer to the capital lived better. My hometown of Joppa was a bustling but crime-ridden seaport town. Its people and businesses were transient, involved in moving legal and illegal things in and out of the port to the capital and elsewhere. This attracted a bad element of people and businesses. The farther away one got from Joppa, the better one's life was. Away from Joppa, good jobs abounded, and there were places to buy things. And people laughed. I hadn't experienced much laughter in my adult life.

At my new job I found myself drawn to a pleasant young woman named Nyah, whose laugh was music. Her break from the checkout line came when I was clocking out. I would linger in the break area to be near her before I left for home. She never seemed to notice me, but I stayed, anyway, to overhear conversations before I left.

Nothing in the break room banter hinted that Nyah had a boyfriend, so I kept up my hopes.

Nyah was always encouraging her workmates, who had all the usual problems. Then one day, Nyah asked the group, "Did I tell you my grandfather doesn't have Parkinson's anymore?"

One girl cried out, "Not the grandfather you've been saying might die soon?"

Nyah replied, "Yes, the bedridden grandfather we feared was dying."

"That's wonderful," said another worker. "Did he get into a new program at the hospital?"

"No, no! Nothing like that," Nyah said. "A man named Peter made

Grandpa well. Peter is a preacher who traveled with the healer, Jesus. And he's one of those who saw Jesus alive after his death."

The first girl objected. She said, "Jesus is dead. His followers stole his body so they could claim he came back to life."

But a guy said, "I disagree. I heard Jesus preach, once, and I saw him heal people. It wasn't fake; it was real. And I believe he could have come back from the dead."

The first girl rolled her eyes. She didn't believe Nyah or Jerry.

To Jerry, Nyah said, "Before Jesus died, I wished for him to come and heal Grandpa. And after I heard he came back to life, I wished, again, that he would come."

The girl said, "You're such a dreamer, Nyah. You want everything to always turn out right. But it doesn't."

At that Nyah replied, "But things have turned out right! That's what I'm trying to tell you."

Nyah said, "A neighbor brought Peter to our home. We told Peter about Grandpa's Parkinson's and how in the last several years he had become bedridden and senile. And Peter asked to go into Grandpa's room. We took him, and Peter stood by Grandpa's bed and said, 'Anaeus. Jesus Christ makes you well. Get up, now, and make your sick bed. You won't need it anymore.'

"Grandpa's eyes flew open, and he looked around the room. Peter helped Grandpa stand, and Grandpa chuckled, as he used to. Then, without a hint of tremor, Grandpa reached over and yanked the sheets and blankets from the bed to the floor. 'Get these washed, Jemma!' he ordered with a giggle. He added, 'But I won't need them until bedtime, tonight.' My mother cried with joy as she picked them up.

"Grandpa next grabbed my hands and danced me around the room. With a sparkle in his eye. He said, 'If you expect me to dance at your wedding, child, you'd better hurry and get married!'

"My family has been celebrating, ever since!"

Some workers in the break room looked doubtful about the healing. But Nyah assured them it was true.

She said, "I only wish I had a car and could go over to Lydda, tomorrow after work, to hear Peter preach. My brother has taken our family car on a business trip. My parents and Grandpa are already in Lydda with friends. I hate missing it all."

I heard myself say, "I could drive you there."

Nyah turned and noticed me for, perhaps, the first time. "How kind," she said. "I may take you up on your offer."

But then, the supermarket manager burst into the break room. "Break's over!" she thundered, and everyone scampered back to their posts.

The woman gave me a stern look when I didn't rush off. I mumbled, "My shift is over; I stock shelves."

"Well," she commanded, "be off with you, then!"

I flashed her a grin and took my leave.

My heart sprouted wings! During my shift, the next afternoon, I dreamed of when Nyah's shift would end. Lydda was only twenty minutes from work. But twenty minutes was twenty minutes. I would have twenty heavenly minutes with Nyah to myself in the car.

I was so starry-eyed in dreaming of my trip to Lydda that, in the morning, I didn't notice if Mama displayed warnings about her health. She never complained, and I never imagined she would ever be ill, until I got a phone call at work telling me to hurry home.

When I left my shift undone and drove up to the house, I found the stoop surrounded by neighbors. Everyone was in tears. They patted my back as I passed through them. My heart pounded as I climbed the steps and opened the door.

And then my heart stopped.

Mama lay on the sofa, and it was clear she was no longer breathing. Manny's mom sat next to her and held her lifeless hand.

I hadn't seen Manny's mother since before Manny's death, but Ellen did not prevent me from coming to kiss my mother's cheek. Ellen laid a hand on my shoulder when I kneeled by the sofa.

"She collapsed on the stairs outside," Ellen said. "We brought her in here. We called for an ambulance, but it hasn't come yet. But it doesn't matter because she's already gone."

Now Ellen wept. And I sobbed with my head on Mama's breast. How could this be true? How could it have happened in such a short time? Why hadn't the ambulance gotten here faster? And why couldn't I have been here? What was happening to the people in my life? First Manny, and now my mother. Was God punishing me? If so, why didn't he take me and not Manny and Mama? My guilt stifled my breathing.

I turned at the sound of familiar voices at the door.

"We're friends of Sol's from work," I heard Nyah say.

Could it be? Was Nyah here? Who had brought her? I knew she didn't have a car.

And then I heard Jerry's voice over my shoulder. "We tried to catch you when we learned you had to leave," Jerry told me. "The manager announced you had gotten a call that something was wrong at home. She said it sounded serious. We went to her office and told her we were both feeling sick and needed to leave. I didn't think she would understand and let us go, but after frowning a lot and muttering under her breath, she looked us up and down and growled 'you'd better be back tomorrow!' We assured her we would be at work tomorrow, and then we tried to catch up to you on the highway. But we lost you."

Nyah knelt beside me and touched my hand. "I'm sorry, Sol," she said. And I cried into her shoulder. Grief thwarted what should have been a blissful moment in Nyah's arms. Joy was impossible in the face of death.

Jerry extended his condolences and sat for a few minutes. Then he left. "I'll be back," he said. "I have to go to Lydda."

I wasn't thinking, or I would have asked why he needed to go to Lydda, right now; couldn't it wait?

Through the door Jerry had opened to leave, people from the front of the house filed in to pay their respects.

Widowed mothers with little ones clinging to their legs crept in and left their caresses and remembrances. "Thank you, friend," one lady said. And even though my mother's eyes could not see, she said, "See how little Sarah's coat fits her?"

An elderly man with a cane placed his hand over mine as he said, "Thank you, Dorcas, for the soup you brought when I was sick."

An old, half-blind widow bowed in prayer. "Thank you, Dorcas. If you hadn't paid my utility bill this winter, I know I would have died."

I marveled when one of the user's I had sold drugs to cried at her feet, "Thank you for knitting me socks when I was too stoned to buy them this winter and my feet were freezing."

Over and over, the tributes came, and I marveled at all the things my mother had done. She was only one woman, but she had affected scores of lives. I experienced shame. My need of her paled against the needs of those in our little community. My silent cry became, *how will WE cope without you, Mama?*

Before the line of mourners was half through with their visits to my mother's side, I heard a siren. The long-overdue ambulance edged its way through the crowded street and up to the curb in front of the house. Two EMTs raced up the stairs. At the top, one of them asked, "Where is the woman we got the call about?"

The crowd derided them with, "Where've you been! You're late!"

"We're sorry," said the man, "We received two calls at the same time. We've come as quickly as we could."

The heckler replied, "Well, I hope you were able to help the other person. This person's died."

I hurried to the door and let the EMTs into the house and into the living room. The first moved to the sofa and bent to examine Mama's body. He felt her coldness and lifted her lifeless eyelids. He put his stethoscope to her chest and stood.

"I'm sorry," he said, again. "We really did try to get here, sooner."

I sighed. It had been over an hour. I wondered if the other call had been for someone in a good part of town. I tried not to think the EMTs might have put a lesser value on my mother's call because of our poor neighborhood.

And then, there was another commotion on the porch steps. Someone commented: "It's Peter, the healer! Too bad he's too late, too."

Peter, the healer? Nyah had talked about him, yesterday, healing her grandfather. Why was Peter here? Had someone brought him who didn't know Mama had died?

I heard laments to Peter that if he had been here sooner, he could have healed Mama. Our neighbors made sure he knew Dorcas had been their friend and helped them pay bills and keep warm. Some showed off the clothes and socks she had made and told of the blankets she had distributed in cold weather. Others described the soup she had brought when they were sick.

Before I could get to the door to meet and rescue Peter from everyone's need to share their loss, I heard Jerry's voice.

"In here," Jerry said. "She's in here."

It caught me by surprise. Had Jerry brought Peter? But why? My mother had been dead when Jerry left the house.

Now, Jerry said, "This is my friend, Sol, and this is his mother, Dorcas."

At sight of Peter, the mourners in the living room took up where those on the steps had left off in telling how Dorcas had blessed them.

"She was a good woman," one cried. "There is no one left, now, to help us."

An elderly man said, "At one time we had only the cast-off clothing the religious council collects."

And a middle-aged woman added, "The things Dorcas made were better than store-bought."

All the while, a younger woman wept. "Where will I get food to feed my family, tonight?" she cried. "My babies will go hungry."

The need stifled me. How had my mother helped so many people?

Peter raised his hands and said to those in the room, "Thank you for sharing. But now, we need to clear this room. Can you wait outside for a few minutes?"

The room emptied, and Jerry whispered in my ear, "This is the man who knows Jesus. I asked Peter to come because I believe he can do something."

Do something? I wondered, *what did 'do something' mean? My mother was dead. The only thing left to do was to bury her.*

I wanted to thank Jerry and send him and Peter on their way. But I didn't because of Nyah.

Peter crossed the room to the sofa, and I fought an impulse to say, it was nice of you to come, but there's nothing here to heal.

I watched Peter kneel beside Mama and begin to pray. I prayed, too, a prayer of despair.

Oh, God! I cried in silence. *Why did Mama have to die?*

With my head still bowed, I heard Peter stand. Perhaps he was leaving, now.

I stood to bid him well.

But Peter did not move. He stood over my mother's body. And then, he spoke—not to us standing behind him, but to her. To Mama.

"Okay, Tabitha," Peter said. "You can get up, now."

How did he know my mother's name was Tabitha? Few people knew that. Everyone called her *Dorcas*, but this stranger had called her by her given name.

As I contemplated this and his words to her, my mother's eyelids fluttered.

My legs buckled. I was imagining things! I must be. Mama is dead. The EMTs confirmed it, and I had felt her cold lips.

But in the next moment, Mama's eyes opened!

Peter stood above her, and she saw his face and smiled.

Then, as if Mama felt guilty for lying down with guests present, she sat up and patted her hair, as I had seen her do a thousand times after a nap.

Her cheeks glowed with the blush of life, and I raced to kiss her.

"Mama!" I cried. Still sitting, she embraced me and whispered, "Solly!"

Peter reached for her hand in what looked like an invitation to dance, and Mama nodded and stood. She and Peter walked to the door, and Peter opened it to present my mother alive to those who waited.

At first, our neighbors doubted what they saw. Then one person gave a shout, and another, and another. And the street exploded with joy and praise and swaying and handkerchiefs waved overhead. Cell phones captured Mama and Peter and the exuberant celebration and sent the pictures all over town.

A bald man began to chant, *"Make a joyful noise, I say, unto the Lord, all ye 'hoods in all the land!"* And the familiar chorus, drawn from Psalm 100, burst from the lips of the dancers with such sheer joy that I laughed to think this was the same crowd who had come weeping and wailing, earlier.

Mama strutted like a rock star on the top step and clapped over her head to God. "Thank you, God!" she shouted. "Thank you!"

This was church as I recalled it from my youth. Years ago, while others had praised, I had gone through the motions. But, today, my praise, like theirs, was real!

And the celebration spread to friends and family beyond the neighborhood, and the dancing wove through the side streets and onto a major thoroughfare. The police wondered who had won a ballgame, and they blocked off the street until the dancing could subside.

Mama shouted to those still around the porch at the house, "You need to go home and get your families fed and taken care of. I'll still be here tomorrow—I promise! And Tyra, I'll bring you soup in a little while for you and your babies."

A large woman, who lived next door, shouted louder. "Scat, you all!" she ordered. "Go home! Dorcas needs her rest, don't you think? She's been through a lot today."

And although the dancing continued beyond our street, our immediate neighborhood settled. The last to go was Angel Ragland, who twirled her handmade dress for Mama.

"See!" she cried, "It's so pretty, and I love it!" Then she danced after her mother, down the street.

Mama laughed, and Ellen and I drew Mama inside and begged her to sit.

It was then I realized Jerry and Nyah had disappeared—probably to return Peter to Lydda. The only people left in the room were me, my mother, Manny's mother Ellen, and the two EMTs.

I had forgotten the EMTs. Their vehicle had been trapped by the celebration, and I expected them to be angry. Instead, they were torn between disbelief and astonishment. They had seen Mama awaken after Peter's prayer.

I invited them to examine Mama. ("Since you're here," I said.)

When the men approached her, I read their faces. How do you examine a miracle? How do you write it up, back at the hospital?

The EMTs took Mama's pulse and heart rate and looked into her irises. They touched her bare arms and listened to her breathing.

Then, one of them said, "Who was that man?"

I answered, "His name is Peter." And I repeated what I had learned from Nyah: "He was a close friend and associate of Jesus, the healer."

The EMT said, "I never would have believed this could be possible. The hospital staff is going think we're crazy. This the most miraculous thing I've ever seen."

I remembered that Peter would be in Lydda for a few days, and I suggested to the EMT, "You can go to Lydda and hear Peter and maybe see him heal others."

"I will!" said the younger man. "I will go hear him. And if he heals people like this, I have a couple of seriously ill patients I plan to take with me!"

The EMTs looked at each another, and, at the same time, they said, "Jared and Cecily!" Then they laughed and said an excited goodbye. I got the impression that two very sick people—Jared and Cecily—would soon be riding to Lydda in a racing ambulance.

No sooner had the EMTs left than there was a knock on the door.

"Channel 4 News," the reporter announced.

Within a half hour, the broadcast of the raising of Dorcas filled the airwaves.

That miraculous day was long ago. And Mama continues to pray for me. She also prays for Nyah and our children. And we all pray for Grandfather and Nyah's parents. (And yes, Grandpa danced at our wedding!)

Together, we have ministered to our neighbors in Joppa and Emmaus with food and clothing and money to pay bills. And we celebrate Mama's return to life.

We also celebrate that when the death of our earthly bodies (including Mama's) comes, we can trust the power of Jesus to give us new life—everlasting life.

Mama's raising was an example, a taste of what is to come. Our permanent life—not just this temporary existence—lies ahead of us, with Jesus.

Thank you, Lord, for living, dying, rising again, and preparing our awakening into your glorious eternity!

12

SCOTT'S STORY: HIS TIMELESS TOUCH STILL CHANGES LIVES

Two thousand years have elapsed since Jesus walked the earth. And I thrill to the stories of his message, miracles, and marvelous grace.

On days when my bones ache and my body fails me, I wish I could brush the hem of his garment or wait in the long line seeking his healing touch. His healings were so complete I would not need the handful of pills I consume each day—pills that would be miracles to his contemporaries.

Prayers have brought me relief and added skill to surgeons' hands, many times in my life. And I am grateful for these blessings. But, like Bartimaeus, Jairus's daughter, the demon-possessed Syrophoenician, and others, these miracles are temporary. Even Lazarus, whom Jesus raised from the dead, has gone again to his grave.

But Jesus's healings and raisings were proof he was who he said he was: the son of God. And he took our infirmities on himself—infirmities germinated in the rebellion of Adam and Eve against God—and Jesus buried them in a grave for three days. But the tomb could not hold him. He conquered sin and death. And because Jesus lives, he can call our souls from the grave to begin a new life with him, forever.

And we needn't wait before we can feel his touch. He has sent his spirit, the holy spirit, to live within us and guide us in our earthly walk. When we invite Jesus into our hearts, he transforms us to know him better and to glimpse our eternal purpose. Then he helps us to achieve it.

We can:

- Lose our doubt like Thomas.
- Catch visions of Jesus's eternal godhead, like John.
- Experience freedom from sins that defeat us, like the woman caught in adultery.
- See the face of our healer and follow him, like the blind beggar.
- Correct the mistakes of our lives, like the height-challenged tax collector.
- Rise up to serve, like Peter's mother-in-law.
- Claim victory over evil, like the Syrophoenician's daughter.
- Put behind us old traditions and put on truth, like the religious leaders who came to Jesus at night or fell on their knees to beg insight.
- Trust his grace, like the thief on the cross.
- And more.

That's the kind of touch Jesus has brought to my life since I met him.

I encountered God when I was twenty-two. I had rebelled from an emotionally difficult childhood and had embarked on my own path, away from the control and expectations of others. Bar tending had offered what I had believed was the best of all worlds. I fled to Old Town Chicago to master it. But God sought me out. I didn't even know who he was, but he pursued me.

By a unique vision of his love, God directed me to enroll in a Christian college. There, a student introduced me to Jesus and shared the plan of salvation.

Like many characters in the New Testament, I had not been aware my soul was in jeopardy. But when I met Jesus, I came face-to-face with my sin and my need of healing. And from across the centuries and across the divide between heaven and earth, Jesus touched me. I confessed and asked him to forgive and cover my sins with his shed blood on the cross. And he healed my soul for eternity.

Not long after my spiritual rebirth, I met Debby, a woman who had grown up with the stories of Jesus and had experienced his rebirth, as I had. And we fell in love and married.

God then led me into church ministry, and I pastored for over forty years. I thrilled to be able to introduce Jesus to seeking souls and to teach and baptize in his name.

One day, my tired, old body will give out. But I know a perfect one awaits. Jesus promises it! On that day, I will join a company of thousands—no, millions—from across the pages of time, who have been touched by the son of God and the healer of souls.

And on that day, I will see what John saw in his revelation vision—Jesus in his full majesty as king of heaven and earth. And I will offer a worship deeper than any I've given this side of heaven.

Every broken thing in creation will be made whole, every hurt will be healed, and time will be no more.

Debby and I pray you will discover Jesus as your soul-healer. Believe Jesus is who he says he is: the one and only son of God, who took on an earthly body to show us there is more to life than pain and brokenness. Learn about him and ask Jesus into your heart.

One day, I hope to meet you inside the gates of heaven where we can share our stories of his timeless touch.

Notes From The Author

I believe if Jesus had come in our day, our reactions would have been no different from those in Biblical times. Some would experience his healing and follow him and others would condemn him to death. In my stories, I have concentrated on those who followed him. Each one experienced a life change due to a healing encounter with the son of God, and each story ends with a yearning for his return to permanently heal the world.

I hope my stories spur a kingdom longing in you and help remind you of the hope you and I have in Jesus.

Like his early followers, we do not know what the immediate future holds, and we have no guarantee that there will not be great cost in following him. But as Paul says in 2 Timothy 1:12 (KJV):

> *...I know whom I have believed and am persuaded that he is able to keep that which I have committed unto him against that day.*

Hebrews 10:25 (KJV) tells us to exhort and encourage one another, *"and so much more, as ye see the day approaching."*

And so, my stories are written to exhort and encourage. Believe, my friend! Jesus did live. Jesus does live. And Jesus is coming again.

Someone has said, "Christ didn't stay dead, and he won't stay gone!" Holding fast to this truth will become more precious as difficulties arise. As did his early followers, we will begin to scan the skies before it is all done. And we will ask, "Is that his cloud I see?"

Is That His Cloud I See?

When things were good, I failed to peek;
I seldom longed, I didn't seek.
I seldom stopped to scan the skies
Or wonder when the saints might rise.

I never thought to search the sun.
But now, the time has come.
I scan the skies more longingly:
When will His Coming Cloud I see?

Weary, scourged, and forced to hide,
His battered saints have bled and died.
All slaughtered are His little lambs,
Who rest now in His heavenly hands.

So, now at last, I long to gasp:
"Is that perchance His trumpet blast?
Are those His wings above the trees?
Is that? Is that His Cloud I see?"

DEBBY L. JOHNSTON

Scripture Index

Here are Scripture accounts that formed the basis for each story:

1 - Part of His Company (Matthew 4-28; John 20)

Part One

Disciples called: Mt 4:18-22
Sick healed: Mt 4:23-25
Waves stilled: Mt 8:23-27, Mk 4:36-41, Lk 8:22-25
Twelve sent out: Mt 10:1-11:1
Twelve couldn't heal boy: Mt 17:14-21
Boy's lunch multiplied by Jesus: Jn 6:1-15
Crowd wants to crown Jesus king: Jn 6:14-15
Walking on water: Mt 14:22-33, Mk 6:47-51, Jn 6:15-21
Feed 4000: Mk 8:1-11, Mt 15:29-38
Lazarus raised: Jn 11:1-44
Jesus's claim to be the resurrection and the life: Jn 11:25-26
Plots against Jesus: Jn 12:20-36
Jesus accused of healing by the Devil: Mt 16:23, Mk 8:31-9:1, Lk 9:22-27
Attempts to stone Jesus: Jn 8:58-59, Jn 10:30-31
Triumphal entry into Jerusalem: Mt 21:1-11, Lk 19:29-38, Jn 12:12-15
A parable against the religious leaders: Mt 23:1-39
Trial and Death: Mt 26:14-27:65, Mk 10 & 11 & 14 & 15, Lk 22:3-6 & 23, Jn 18 & 19 & 20

Part Two

Alive again: Mt 28:1-15, Lk 24, Jn 20
Mary Magdalene: Lk 8:2, Mt. 27:55-56
Jesus appears without Thomas: Jn 21:19-23
Appears to Thomas: Jn 21:24-29
Later appearances: Jn 21, Acts 1:1-11
Awaiting new Heaven and new Earth: Isa 65:17 & 66:22, Rev 21:1

2 - Visions (John 6:1-15; Revelation 1:10-17)

Boy's Lunch: Jn 6:1-15
Jairus: Mk 5:22-43, Lk 8:41-56
Twelve sent out: Mt 10:1-11:1
Twelve couldn't heal boy: Mt 17:14-21
Request to sit on Jesus right and left: Mt 20:20-23, Mk 10:35-45
Transfiguration: Mt 17:1-9, Mk 8:2-10
Trial and Death: Mt 26:14-27:65, Mk 10 & 11 & 14 & 15, Lk 22:3-6 & 23, Jn 18 & 19 & 20
Lazarus raised from the dead: Jn 11:1-44
Jesus raises the son of a widow from Nain: Lk 7:11
Elisha raises Shunammite woman's son from the dead: 2 Kings 4:34-36
Appears to Thomas: Jn 21:24-29
Later appearances: Jn 21, Acts 1:1-11
John's Visions: Rev 1:10-17

3 - Set Free (John 8:2-11)

John the Baptist: Mt 3:1-17, Mk 1:3-13, Lk 3:2-17

4 - Dreams (Luke 18:35-42, Mt 10:29-34, Mk 10:46-52)

5 - Standing Tall (Luke 19:1-9)

6 - Mother-In-Law (Luke 4:38-39, Mt 8:14-15, Mk 1:29-31)

Peter's call to be a disciple: Lk 5:1-11
Peter's wife may have traveled with him after Pentecost: I Cor 9:5

7 - Payment (Matthew 17:24-27)

Turn cheek: Mt 5:39, Lk 6:29
Calling authorities "brood of vipers": Mt 12:33-37
Widows cheated: Mt 23:14, Mk 12:40, Lk 20:47
Jesus knows thoughts: Mt 12:25, Lk 5:22
Peter proclaims Jesus as the Christ, the Son of God: Mt 16:16
Jesus knows events (unridden colt): Mt 21:2
Jesus knows events (upper room available): Mt. 14:15
Jesus knows events (woman at well): Jn 4:17
Nets full: Lk 5:1-11
Get behind me, Satan: Mt 16:22-23, Mk 8:33
God is our Father who cares for us: Mt. 6:26

8 - Crumbs (Mark 7:24-30)

Demons speaking, elsewhere in Scripture: Lk 8:26-37

9 - All I Own (Mark 10:17-27)

Cana wedding: Jn 2:1-10
Judging: Mt 7:1-5
Narrow gate: Mt 7: 13-14
False teachers: Mt 7:15-27
Jesus taught with authority: Mt 7:28-29
Jesus healed after teaching: Mt 8:16-17
Pharisees plotting: Mt 12:14, Mk 10:2-12
Old Testament miracles (Moses and plagues): Ex 7-11
Old Testament miracles (Sun stood still): Josh 10:12

Old Testament miracles (Daniel in lion's den): Dan 6:7, I Ki 18:25

Jesus's prayer, "Father you always hear me": Jn 11:42

Praise Psalm: **Ps 103 (quoted from KJV)**

Need more righteousness than Pharisees: Mt 5:20

Jesus accused of healing by the Devil: Mt 16:23, Mk 8:31-9:1, Lk 9:22-27

Get right with others before sacrifice: Mk 11:25 (cp Dt 15:7-11)

Don't swear: Mt 5:34 (cp Lev 19:12, Dt 23:23)

Love enemies, no revenge: Mt 5:44-48, Lk 6:27 (cp Lev 4:20 & 19:18, Pv 25:8-10)

Don't worry: Mt 6:25-34 (cp Ps 23)

Love mercy: **Micah 6:8**

None holy or good but God: I Sa 2:2

God is One God: Dt 6:4

Ten commandments: Ex 20:1-17

Great commandments: Mt 22:37, Mk 12:30, Lk 10:27 (cp Dt 6:5 & 10:12. Lev 19:18, Dt 10:18-19

Seek first righteousness, & don't worry: **Mt 6:33-34 (quoted from KJV)** (cp Pv 3:5-6)

Pluck out eye: Mt 5:29

Triumphal entry into Jerusalem: Mt 21:1-11, Lk 19:29-38, Jn 12:12-15

Hosanna: Ps 118:25-26

Speaking against Pharisees: Mt 21-23

Lament over Jerusalem: Mt 23:37

Trial and Death: Mt 26:14-27:65, Mk 10 & 11 & 14 & 15, Lk 22:3-6 & 23, Jn 18 & 19 & 20

Temple veil torn: Mt 27:51

Alive again: Mt 28:1-15, Lk 24, Jn 20

Emmaus appearance: Lk 24:13

Lazarus raised: Jn 11:1-44

Jesus appears without Thomas: Jn 21:19-23

Sold all: Acts 5:34

10 - Mercy (Luke 23:40-43)

Beatitudes: Mt 5-6 (**Mt 5:3-5 quoted from KJV**)
Storing treasures: Mt 6:19-24
Jesus taught with authority: Mt 7:28-29
Jesus speaks against authorities: Lk 20
Two thieves crucified with Jesus: Lk 23:33
Religious leaders were at the crucifixion: Lk 23:35
Jesus forgives His crucifiers: **Lk 23:34 (quoted from KJV)**
Taunt with "if you are God, then heal yourself": Lk 23:35-39
Thief to be with Jesus in Paradise: Lk 23:40-43

11 - For the Love (Acts 9:36-42)

Peter healed Aeneas: Acts 9:32-35
Praise: Psalm 100 (**Psalm 100:1 quoted from KJV**)

12 - Scott's Story: His Timeless Touch Still Changes Lives

Believe: John 1:11-12
Blessed are those who have never seen Him and yet believe: John 20:29
John's Revelation vision: Revelation 1
Jesus has prepared a place for us: **John 14:1-3 (quoted from KJV)**

BIBLE CHARACTER INDEX

Here are the Bible characters that have formed the basis for each story:

1 - Part of His Company – Thomas, the Disciple

2 - Visions – The lad whose lunch Jesus divided to feed the five thousand; John, the Disciple

3 - Set Free – The woman caught in adultery

4 - Dreams – Bartimaeus

5 - Standing Tall – Zacchaeus

6 - Mother-In-Law – Simon Peter's mother-in-law

7 - Payment – Simon Peter, the Disciple

8 - Crumbs – The Syrophoenician woman

9 - All I Own – The rich, young ruler

10 - Mercy – Thief on the Cross

11 - For the Love – Dorcas and Simon Peter, the Disciple

12 - Scott's Story: His Timeless Touch Still Changes Lives – Those who never saw the Lord and yet have believed

ABOUT THE AUTHOR

God's desire has always been to draw us to himself. And in so doing, he is sometimes surprising, sometimes stern, but always loving. I find it marvelous how he transforms broken lives into whole and holy children. I started my writing late in life, which allows me to draw characters and anecdotes from my years of personal Bible study and experience as a minister's wife. While my stories are fictionalized, they are drawn from truth and are woven into the broader tapestry of God at work through his son, Jesus. Jesus still reaches out with his timeless touch to redeem and change lives for eternity. Learn more at _www.DebbyLJohnston.com_ and on Facebook at Debby L. Johnston.

Debby L. Johnston

Book One—where the Cherish series begins!

Cherish: A Still, Small Call is the first book in author Debby L. Johnston's Christian fiction series about Reverend Andy Garrett and his family. Read the story of Andy's past—a surprising past. Get a peek at the difficulties of Andy's childhood, but also uncover his dramatic conversion and the positive influences of people like Grannie who prayed for him; the gorgeous ninth-grade teacher, Miss Randall, who spurred him to read; and a college friend named Bonnie who helped him to open the Bible. Learn how Andy met and pursued Abbey Preston, the love of his life. Then follow Andy's call to serve the Cherish First Baptist Church—the endearing small-town ministry that God had in mind for him all the time!

Book Two—joys and tears bring you closer to Cherish and the Garrett family.

Cherish: Behold, I Knock continues the story begun in the first *Cherish* novel, about Reverend Andy Garrett, his family, his friends, and the working of God in the quaint rural community of Cherish. Andy grows as a minister, despite bats in the sanctuary, a deaf substitute pianist, a wild-haired and poetic church secretary, and a baptistry that boils over the night before a baptism. Andy also learns how his unchurched, bar-tending background was part of God's plan to change the life of a drug-addicted teen. Most of all, Andy finds an opportunity to share with his own parents the love of God and the truth of Christ's redemption. The story of *Cherish: Behold, I Knock* reveals a remarkable God at work in drawing the broken and the broken-hearted to Himself.

CHERISH:
Create in Me a Clean Heart

DLJ

Number Three in the Cherish Series
Debby L. Johnston

Book Three—the Cherish experience deepens, and surprises delight!

In *Cherish: Create in Me a Clean Heart* you'll get your farm boots dirty. The farmers of Reverend Andy Garrett's church in Cherish have teased him about being a city boy, but they nod approvingly after he helps deliver a litter of pigs, relieve a constipated draft horse, and tip a cow with a displaced stomach. These things prove to be simple, however, compared to a challenge Andy had never expected—the challenge of pastoring his father, a man who has cursed God all his life. Thankfully, Christ faithfully draws Mac Garrett closer to Himself, and He miraculously closes the divide between father and son.

Abounding with characters you've come to love—and new ones you'll delight to meet—*Cherish: Create in Me a Clean Heart* inspires, as well as surprises, with tears and laughter.

READER'S DISCUSSION GUIDE

One - PART OF HIS COMPANY

1. No one knows why Thomas wasn't with the other disciples when Jesus first appeared to them. It is pure speculation that he went back home. He may have been grieving, or he may have refused to hide away.

2. While it is likely Jesus healed people in Thomas's hometown, there is no direct Scripture to support an event like the one I have portrayed. By including this as an aspect in my story, however, I have been able to provide possible emotions Thomas felt about Jesus's healings and how Thomas might have been changed by the experience.

3. In Jesus's day and place, there were no buses, of course. Walking and ship travel were common. If Jesus had lived today, it is more likely he would have traveled in a motorized vehicle, so I have given him and his disciples a bus. And who better to drive than Peter, and who to pay for the gas than Judas?

4. What would it have been like to be able to heal as Jesus commanded his disciples? The Twelve (even Judas!) must have been in as much amazement to be given Jesus's healing power as the people they were sent to minister to.

5. Leprosy is not a commonly dreaded disease in our day, as it was in Jesus's day, but we can relate to HIV and the fear of contamination from it, so I have included HIV instead of leprosy in my dreaded disease example for Thomas to heal.

6. To the Twelve, it must have seemed, at times, as if Jesus was sending them mixed messages. On the one hand he told them, "I'm the son of God," but in the next breath (so to speak) he said, "I'm going to die." How does one put those two statements together? Surely, God cannot die.

7. The prelude to Jesus's resurrection was the raising of Lazarus. No doubt Lazarus and his sisters hid out with the disciples after the death of Jesus.

8. When Jesus is arrested and killed, the world turns upside down for the disciples, including Thomas. Until Jesus appears to them, they must have wondered what to do and where to go.

9. What mixed stories must have circulated about Jesus's resurrection until his appearances confirmed what was true! Today, we would have 24/7 news coverage with interviews and much speculation.

10. Mary Magdalene's healing from seven demons is mentioned but not described in Scripture. I drew from stories of other demonic healings in imagining what it must have been like for her.

11. When Jesus appeared to the disciples (the first time, when Thomas was absent), we read in Mark 16:11 that he scolded them for not believing the reports from the women and the travelers to Emmaus. Perhaps Thomas was scolded, too, but Scripture seems to show Jesus going out of his way to reassure Thomas and to dispel his doubts.

12. While it is not impossible, there is no Scripture telling us the disciples disguised themselves and saw the body of Jesus as it was transported to the tomb. I have included this idea to lend credence to Thomas's belief that Jesus was truly dead, and to wonder if he still bore the marks of his cruel torture.

13. Jesus's final words give purpose and hope to his disciples, and the holy spirit gives each the boldness and power to go forward—even to one who had doubted.

Two – VISIONS

1. Unlike the other disciples, John was not martyred. Instead, he was imprisoned on the penal island of Patmos where it is likely he worked in the prison mines. And he lived to old age.

2. We do not know the background of the lad with the loaves and fishes or how the disciples ended up with his lunch. I have invented a food camper for the lad's family—something an enterprising food service would likely do in today's setting if Jesus was traveling about and drawing crowds.

3. It should be obvious I have made up a relationship between John and the lad whose lunch Scripture says played a part in the feeding of the 5,000. By inventing a relationship between the two, it gives me an audience for John as he relates his past and his vision.

4. My story of Jairus follows Scripture fairly closely, and Scripture gives us many details with this account. I have pulled in additional imagined details that are probably not far from the actual story.

5. John and his brother James had no idea what they were asking when they wanted to be seated on Jesus's right and left when he came into his kingdom. I have imagined John revisiting that request once he sees the risen Jesus in his rightful realm. John would likely be appalled to think he had once asked Jesus such a thing!

6. I have gladly taken advantage of the many details Scripture has given us about the transfiguration of Jesus. In our modern day, I fear we are less impressed with the transfiguration vision than the disciples were in Jesus's day, because we view the transfiguration through the lens of Hollywood portrayals of time travel, quantum leaps, and super heroes.

7. In my story I allude briefly to the fear that kept the disciples in hiding and then the boldness that came upon them after the holy spirit filled them. Sadly, although I possess the holy

spirit, I am ashamed I often lack the boldness these first believers expressed. What a difference their testimony has made through the ages!

8. John's reaction to seeing the risen Christ in his full glory can scarcely be imagined. That vision—even second-hand—should make us bold and eager to serve until our Lord comes again!

Three - SET FREE

1. We have no Scriptural background to draw from for the woman caught in adultery. She may have been a victim. Or she may have been an instigator. Sadly, sexual sin—whether in Jesus's day or our day—entraps and enslaves men and women, and it prevents and destroys healthy marriage relationships.

2. John the Baptist not only seems strange by our modern standards, but he was also strange in his own day. There was no one like him because no one else had been called in the way he had. He was the embodiment of the prophets of old and dressed and acted like them.

3. In Scripture it is the religious leaders who bring the adulterous woman to Jesus for condemnation. In my story I've put the news reporters in that role. Either way, the idea was to entrap Jesus with whatever decision he might make. But Jesus engages in an activity that turns the tables on them. In Scripture, Jesus writes an undisclosed message on the ground; in my story he sends an undisclosed message by cell-phone text. Either way, what Jesus said and whatever he wrote silenced those who had been calling for judgment. Jesus then displays mercy and calls for the accused to go and sin no more.

4. In Scripture, the adulterer is not mentioned and is presumed to be absent when the adulteress is accused and brought to Jesus. Women were treated unequally in that setting. However, in the modern setting of my story, it would be more

likely the adulterer would be accused and brought to Jesus, too. So, I have written this into my story.

5. In Scripture we do not know if the woman's husband was present when she was brought to Jesus. I have added him to my story so we can see a possible outcome of Jesus's command to "go and sin no more."

6. Also, in other New Testament contexts, when Jesus says "your sins are forgiven," there is always an inner healing that takes place. I have taken the liberty to assume the adulterous woman is cleansed of her deceitful heart's bent toward seduction.

Four – DREAMS

1. In our day, blindness carries less of the desperation of trying to support oneself than would have been true in Jesus's day. Those who were blind in that day were usually consigned to begging to support themselves in the most meager way. It is hard for us, today, to imagine that a blind person could not make a good living, or live in their own home, or move about without assistance. I've pictured Bartimaeus in a more modern way, which I hope does not detract from the basic story of Jesus's healing.

2. Although there is nothing to suggest it in Scripture, I have used a dream to facilitate the introduction of Bartimaeus to Jesus. I am reminded of Joel's prophecy of dreams and visions in the latter days (Joel 2:28), and I have heard many missionaries, especially those in Asia, report on the number of converts who are coming to Jesus because of dreams. I believe God can use dreams in anyone's life to get their attention and turn their thoughts toward him. AND when God gives a prophetic vision or dream, he is able to bring it to pass, like he did for Joseph, who interpreted the pharaoh's dream of the famine to come (Genesis 40:14-44).

3. In the Scriptural story (without the dream), there is much more desperation for a blind man. And it is likely Bartimaeus had heard of Jesus's healings, and so, he calls out (bellows) to him in the belief that Jesus is the prophesied messiah, the Son of David, who can heal him—if only he can get Jesus's attention.

4. Often in Scripture, Jesus tells those who are healed to go back to their towns and neighborhoods and share about Christ's healing, there. But in the Scriptural story of Bartimaeus, I like it that Jesus allows the healed man to follow him.

Five - STANDING TALL

1. We are never told why Zacchaeus took up tax collecting. I have speculated that, based on his small stature, he might have been bullied and chose to become a tax collector out of revenge. That theme would hardly be out of the realm of the possible, today.

2. In Scripture we have no tie between Bartimaeus and Zacchaeus. But when I noted they were from the same area, I wondered if Zacchaeus might have, at some time, passed Bartimaeus, as the blind man begged on the side of the road. That led me to bring them together in my story.

3. Revenge can be very lonely. Add to that the unpopular avocation of tax collecting and it is likely that Zacchaeus had few friends. I imagined in my story that the religious leaders of the day saw themselves as a valuable God-ordained buffer between the Roman government and the people, while they saw Zacchaeus as a sinful, money-grubbing traitor.

4. Scripture tells us Zacchaeus was eager to see Jesus. We don't know what caused that feeling in him. It is possible he had heard a great deal about Jesus's teachings from other tax collectors, or he had been amazed by health-stricken tax clients Jesus had

healed. In my story, I have invented the possible scenario that Zacchaeus has heard about Bart's healing.

5. In modern times, Bartimaeus would have to declare his healing so he could be taken off the disability rolls, so I have mentioned that in my story. And he would have to get a job.

6. From our Sunday school childhood most of us have heard the story of Zacchaeus climbing the tree to see Jesus, and we have sung the little chorus that says, "Zacchaeus, you come down! I'm coming to your house today." But we might not have imagined the rush of preparations Zacchaeus would have needed to make in order to get ready to entertain Jesus and those traveling with him.

7. And Scripture doesn't say Zacchaeus waited to get home to make his announcement of restoration to those he has taxed. In my story, I have set that announcement as taking place at Zacchaeus' home, at the dinner table with Jesus. I have speculated on what might have prompted Zacchaeus to make restoration. Scripture does not fill in the details of how Zacchaeus came to his change of heart. Scripture just assumes we understand that it is Jesus who brought Zacchaeus to repentance and stirred him to return what he has unjustly taken in his tax collection role.

Six - MOTHER-IN-LAW

1. Nothing in Scripture tells us Peter's mother-in-law had been against the marriage of her daughter to Peter, but in my story, I have played on a common mother-in-law stereotype that no one is good enough for her daughter.

2. Although Scripture tells us Peter had a boat, or boats, there is, of course, no mention of them having any ownership in a cannery, as I say in my story. Canneries were unheard of in Jesus's day. Most fish were dried or salt-dried. But in today's

terms, Peter might have had some connection with, and maybe part ownership in, a cannery for preserving his catch.

3. There is nothing in Scripture to say Peter had tried to save his widowed mother-in-law's home from foreclosure. Neither does it say the religious establishment purchased it below list price. But Matthew 23:14, Mark 12:40, and Luke 20:47 do imply that it was not unusual for widows to be left homeless by the actions of unscrupulous religious leaders. In any event, the mother-in-law and Peter's wife came to live with Simon and Andrew, according to Mark 1:29.

4. On the occasion of Mark 1:29, Scripture does not say this is the first time Jesus has come to Peter's house, but I have written my story as if this is so. And I have imagined and written that Peter's wife and mother-in-law went out of their way to impress Jesus. And when the mother-in-law became fevered and couldn't help serve, it probably made her feel terrible. In my story, I couldn't resist imagining Jesus sympathizing with her, even as he healed her. (Actually, in Mark's account, we see that Jesus came to the house at the end of the Sabbath day, so there would have been no immediate grand preparations as I have drawn in my story.)

5. I have imagined that the mother-in-law was not only miraculously healed but also miraculously made presentable (gone was the sweaty hair and soaked, wrinkled clothing) for serving her guests. I have presumed that if Jesus could heal, he could also do the rest. After all, God kept the clothes of the Israelites from wearing out for forty years in the wilderness (Deuteronomy 8:4), so it is not too far-fetched to believe he could or would take care of such details.

6. We have no mention in Scripture about how Peter and his wife handled Peter's absences while he traveled with Jesus. In my story, I have speculated (based on I Corinthians 9:5) that Peter's wife (whose name is unknown) traveled with him from time to time after Pentecost.

Seven – PAYMENT

1. In my story, I have taken liberties with what we know of Peter's character to imagine him thinking he would make sure the Temple tribute tax would be paid, with or without Jesus's instruction to do so.
2. In my story, I have drawn a connection between the story of God's tax provision for his son and God's provision for man's (Peter's) debt. This connection is not spelled out in Scripture. In my story, I have imagined Peter making this connection— and I have hinted that the rest of the connection would come with time: i.e., after Jesus's death and resurrection.
3. Scripture does not tell us how the taxes of the other disciples were paid. I assume they each paid their own taxes.
4. In my story, I have imagined Peter's triumphant attitude with the tax collector—complete with a smiley face next to his signature.

Eight – CRUMBS

1. Although Scripture does not tell us the circumstances of how they arrived, we find the Syrophoenician woman and her demon-possessed daughter on foreign soil. I have modernized the story to make the Syrophoenician woman and her demon-possessed daughter the victims of poverty and a drug-oppressed environment. I have imagined them as fleeing and arriving in the capital city (Jerusalem) and trying to make a living there.
2. Today in Asia and elsewhere in the world, drugs have enslaved thousands of people, either directly or indirectly. Human trafficking of men, women, and children is a common way to pay for drug addiction. Missionaries who encounter sex-trafficked victims, especially children who were trafficked from a very

early age, have reported a high-incidence of mental illness and certain incidences of demon-possession. One can only imagine the pain and bitterness that grows in these victims.

3. In my story, I have drawn the demon-possessed behavior of the daughter from various accounts in Scripture (e.g., Luke 8:26-40; Mark 1:24; 17:14-21).

4. From Scripture, we don't know how the Syrophoenician woman heard about Jesus, but we find her coming to him. In my story, I imagine her going to a house where Jesus is having breakfast. And I tie in the analogy of bread and bread crumbs with a piece of toast held in Jesus's hand.

5. We can only imagine what change might take place in a girl when Jesus finally frees her from demon-possession. I have portrayed the daughter's healing as allowing her to regain the innocence of her lost childhood and to have a normal and loving relationship with her mother and future husband.

Nine - ALL I OWN

1. As in all of my stories, I have been somewhat nebulous about places and religious institutions. In no way does this mean I seek to diminish the Scriptural import of the Jews as God's Chosen People or of Jerusalem's and Israel's place in the outworking of God's historical and Scriptural plan.

2. Because there are few empty fields, today, like the fields where Jesus could have gathered with a crowd and preached to thousands, I have postured in my story that he held events at fairgrounds, football fields, and campgrounds.

3. Scripture doesn't say Jesus never lifted his voice.

4. I have invented the background that the rich young ruler had at first wanted to condemn Jesus. It is possible, but not mentioned in Scripture.

5. Nor does it say in Scripture this ruler had a son who was healed by Jesus. It is not out of the realm of possibility, however, so I have made that part of my story.

6. I have consolidated some of Scripture's reports of Jesus's travels and healing encounters and put them into one event: a visit to a nursing home.

7. In my story of the ruler's son and others being healed, I have pulled and paraphrased from several Scripture occasions of what the healed and healer said.

8. It is not unlikely that religious rulers who praised Jesus and followed him were ostracized and eventually had a price put on their heads.

9. In Scripture, the religious authorities *claim* that demon exorcisms by Jesus were the work of the Devil. In my story, I have expanded their claim to include that ALL of Jesus's healings were the work of Satan.

10. It is unusual for a religious ruler to ask anyone how to inherit eternal life because most of them would have believed themselves worthy of it by virtue of being a descendent of Abraham and having kept all the laws. The rich young ruler may have heard Jesus's teaching that a man's righteousness had to exceed that of the scribes and pharisees. And Scripture says he RAN to Jesus to get his answer, so he must have believed Jesus HAD the answer. I have added all of this speculation into my story.

11. I have imagined that the young ruler saw the triumphal entry of Jesus into Jerusalem and knew others who could tell him about the conviction and execution of Jesus.

12. In my story, I have expanded on the Scriptural mention of the unusual darkness at Jesus's death to imagine that Nathan thought the religious leaders associated it with their guilt for crucifying Jesus and that they fled to the Temple to (repent?) and pray.

13. I have imagined that my character Nathan helped to shield followers of Jesus.
14. In my story, I have imagined the Emmaus travelers and Lazarus telling of their experiences for the rich young ruler's benefit.
15. I have imagined the ruler and his son as present when Jesus appears to the disciples.
16. In my story, I have imagined the ruler selling all he had to help the band of Jesus's followers.

Ten – MERCY

1. We have no idea what kind of thieves hung next to Jesus on the Cross, so long ago. In updating my story, I speculate that one could have been a cyber thief.
2. In my story, I have speculated that the repentant thief had at some time heard Jesus speak. And he might have had a girlfriend like Lucy.
3. Because many illnesses mentioned in Scripture are now "curable" by modern medical care, I have introduced in my story other diseases, such as microcephaly.
4. In my story, I have had to validate a death sentence for theft, because in our modern legal system it is unusual for theft, alone, to result in that penalty.

Eleven - FOR THE LOVE

1. There is nothing in Scripture about Dorcas having a son, let alone a drug-dealing, gang-member of a son. I have invented Solly as a way to show Dorcas' character and as a voice for her story.
2. Joppa, where Dorcas is said to have lived, was a seaport. I have speculated that in a modern culture, Joppa's port might have

been of mixed cultures and controlled by gangsters. I have speculated that Dorcas did not live in the wealthier part of what was no doubt a thriving city. According to Scripture, however, we don't know if she was wealthy or poor—only that she was generous to the poor.

3. I have invented a granddaughter for Anaeus, who was healed by Peter in Scripture. And I have exchanged his "palsy" for Parkinson's disease, which is a common affliction in our time. I realize that the Scripture speaks of Anaeus as having been bedridden for eight years, but that may not be common with Parkinson's disease.

4. Today, it would be normal for an ambulance or emergency squad to be called when someone falls deathly ill. So, I have introduced a couple of EMTs to witness Dorcas' death and her coming back to life.

Twelve – SCOTT'S STORY: HIS TIMELESS TOUCH STILL CHANGES LIVES

1. My testimony and my husband's testimony are examples of how the timeless touch of Jesus still changes lives today.

2. Yes, my husband, Scott, was drawn to God by a vision and introduced to Jesus by the testimony of a friend. We praise God for the work of his holy spirit!

3. If you do not yet know the Jesus of the stories I've shared and have a hunger to know him, you are invited to talk to him in a simple prayer, like this:

Lord Jesus, thank you for dying on the cross for my sins. I know I need you. I invite you, now, into my life, and I welcome you as the only one with the power to save me from sin and to make me right with you and my heavenly father. Thank you for forgiving my sins and for giving me your eternal life. Touch every part of me and make me into the person you originally designed me to be.

Thank you for your love and the assurance that you have heard me and have welcomed me as a reborn child of God. Thank you that I can trust you to never leave me or forsake me. Thank you for your Word, the Bible. Help me study it so I can know you better and know your teachings. And help me let you guide my life and witness. Amen.

Now, seek out other Christians to fellowship with. And if you are new to the stories of Jesus and want to look into his Word, you may want to start with the book of John. Then read the other three Gospels: Matthew, Mark, and Luke. Then follow on through the New Testament, and finally, read the Old Testament.

May God bless you, friends!

Printed in the United States
By Bookmasters